HOLD ONTO ME

The Vigilante Hitman, Book 3

KELLY MOORE

Edited by
KERRY GENOVA
Cover Designer
BEST PAGE FORWARD

Kelly Moore

PROLOGUE

Jake

I'm leaning over the motor of a 1976 Camaro I'm working on when the shop phone rings. I jump and smack the back of my head on the hood.

"Damn it," I grumble as I rub the knot that's left behind.

I wipe my hands on the dirty shop rag I had stuffed in my back pocket as I make my way over to the phone.

"Remington Auto Shop."

"Hey, Jake. It's Glenn. How you doing, man?"

I fall down into my chair that sets behind my flat metal desk. "Good. When you coming to pick up the El Camino I finished a week ago?" I ask, looking over at the shiny back vehicle that's taking up space in my garage.

"That's actually what I was calling about. I don't think I'm going to make it down anytime soon. I'm swamped at work."

I sit up suddenly. "I need this thing out of my shop, man."

He takes a deep breath that I can hear over the phone. "I know. That's why I called to ask if you could bring it to me. I'll throw in a good tip for you."

My hand absentmindedly runs through my thick, dark hair while I think it over. I wouldn't mind getting the extra money, especially with a baby on the way. But that also means I would have to take a day off of work to do so. "How much of a tip are we talking? I have work here that needs to be finished."

"How's an extra grand sound?"

"One thousand dollars and I want the money back that I have to put in gas to get there."

"Deal," he agrees.

"All right. It's still early, so I'll bring it up now."

"Perfect. You're a lifesaver. I should be getting home from work around five this evening. What time do you think you'll make it in?"

I look at my watch. It's about a four-hour drive, and I'll need to load my bike up in the back before I leave so I have a way home. "I should be there by then."

I hear him clap his hands together, excited to have his car back. "Awesome, man. Thanks so much. See you soon."

"No problem," I say, hanging up the phone.

I back the El Camino out of the garage and turn it around so I can load up my bike. It takes me a good twenty minutes to get it loaded up and tied down. Before leaving, I head into the house to tell my future wife, Zoe, where I'll be for the day.

I wander through the house until I find her in the kitchen, baking again. We've been together for four years now, and the woman couldn't cook a damn thing. However, once she got pregnant, she's done nothing but bake. Pies, cookies, cakes, you name it, she's baked it. At one point, we had so many baked goods lying around that we had to take some over to my brother's house by the basket full. Brooklyn loved the sugary treats, and so did the kids, but John wasn't all that happy about it. He refuses to eat anything that Zoe cooks ever since he got food poisoning from the undercooked meatloaf she made one night at a family dinner.

"Baking again?" I ask as I come up behind her, wrapping my arms around her to cup her growing belly. I place my chin in the crook of her neck, pressing soft kisses to her jaw.

She giggles and tries wiggling away from me, but I'm not having any of that.

She pushes her blonde hair behind her ear as she spins around in my arms to face me. "These cravings are getting old. I keep baking what I think I want, but by the time it's done cooking, I want something else."

"I have to leave to deliver a car, but how about I fry up some of that fresh fish John and I caught for dinner?"

"Mmm, that sounds amazing actually. Oh, can we make fries and hush puppies too?"

I laugh. "Whatever you want," I say, landing a firm kiss on her lips that makes her take a deep breath. Her growing chest pushes against mine, and suddenly, I forget what I should be doing.

My hands travel from her lower back, down to her ass. I squeeze slightly before pulling her even closer, causing a sweet groan to escape her lips.

She breaks the kiss with a playful smack to my chest. "I thought you had work to do. Plus, I'm going to burn my cookies if you keep distracting me like this."

"All right, you're right." I take a step back. "I won't be home until late, probably nine or ten tonight. Can you wait that long to have dinner?"

She nods. "You know I do nothing but eat anymore. How about I get everything ready. That way, when you come in, all you have to do is fry everything up."

"Sounds perfect. Call me if you need anything." I smack her on the ass as I walk by. I love having my hands on her anytime that I can.

I climb behind the wheel and hit the road a little faster than I should, but I want to hurry back to have dinner with Zoe, and maybe a little bedroom fun.

I make it to Glenn's apartment building at five on the dot. I know he said he wouldn't get off work until five, so I sit in the car and wait for him to pull up.

I watch the traffic that passes in front of me and notice when a black SUV drives into the parking lot.

It pulls around behind me, and I look up into the rearview mirror out of curiosity.

I quickly take my eyes away when someone knocks on the driver's side window. I look over to see Glenn.

Opening the door, I step out. "Hey, you made it," he says, shaking my hand.

"Yeah, just in time."

He begins walking around the car, running his hand on the hood. "How's she run?"

"Purrs like a kitten," I tell him.

He has a wide smile as he finishes his journey around the vehicle. He takes his place in the driver's seat and twists the key. The car roars to life. I laugh when he hits the gas a few times, revving up the engine.

I'm about to move around to the back of the car to unload my bike when I hear the sound of gravel crunching behind me. I turn to look at whoever is approaching, but as soon as I do, I'm hit over the head.

My ears ring, and my vision blurs. Everything goes black.

CHAPTER ONE
John

I close the range for the night and pack up to head home, in a hurry so I can have dinner with my family. After living the life I had, coming home from an honest living and having dinner with my wife and kids is something I look forward to every day. The kids are growing like a weed; John, who we now call L.J., is six, and Jack is four. Not a day goes by that I don't sit back and watch them play, completely amazed that this is my life. I never thought I would get the happy ending after the life I lived.

I walk in the front door, and Jack is playing on the living room floor. She looks up at me with her big blue eyes and giggles. She pushes herself up on her feet and comes running at me screaming, "Daddy!"

I laugh and pick her up, throwing her into the air and catching her. We do this every day. L.J. must have heard the commotion because he comes running into the room, ready to fight. I see him out of the corner of my eye, trying to sneak up on me. I quickly put Jack down and drop to my knees. L.J. runs headlong toward me. I wrap him up in my arms and pull him to my chest. He's kicking and swinging as hard as he can. Finally, I pretend he's too strong for me, and he breaks loose. He doesn't take it easy on me either. I fall to my side from the attack he's giving, and he jumps on me, pinning me to the floor.

"All right, you win. You're too tough for me," I tell him.

He jumps up, holding his arms up above his head. "Still the champion!"

I laugh as I get myself to my feet, ruffling his hair as I make my way to the kitchen to find my beautiful wife.

She's behind the stove, preparing dinner like I knew she would be. I wrap my arms around her stomach and pull her to my chest. "It smells amazing," I whisper into her ear.

"It's your favorite—grilled steak and fresh fish."

"Surf and turf," I say as she spins around in my arms, pressing her lips to mine. This is something I know I will never get enough of.

While the nightmares of being held captive have all faded away, there is still a split second before my eyes open when I think I've lost her for good. In that moment, I'm in a panic almost every morning until I find her lying at my side like she always is.

She smacks another quick kiss on my lips. "How was work?" she asks, pulling away to resume cooking.

I grab a beer from the fridge and pop the top. "Good. Same old, same old," I answer, sitting down and kicking my feet up on the empty chair next to mine.

She places the tongs down on the stovetop and turns around, looking at her feet as her hands hold on to the counter behind her. "John, you're not getting bored, are you?"

"Bored?" I asked, confused.

She nods slowly. "Yeah, you know. Your life used to be fast-paced. It was full of speeding motorcycles, stray bullets, and women. Now..." She shrugs. "Now it's full of screaming kids and the same old wife and job."

I set my beer down on the table and stand, pulling her back against me where she belongs. "I don't ever want you to think that this life with you and the kids isn't enough for me. That life I lived before, it wasn't a life. It was simply surviving. You"—I kiss her nose —"and the kids are it for me. And, I kinda like this old wife." I wink at her.

She softly places her hand against my cheek. "I love you more every day. Have I ever told you that?"

I want to break up the serious tone, so I put my cocky face on. "No, but I can tell because each night in the bedroom you get louder and louder at screaming my name." Slowly, my lips find hers once again.

She pushes me away with a smile. "Shut up and set the table, would ya? I seem to remember you doing the screaming last night." She smirks, then picks up the tongs.

God I love her sassiness. My wicked mind would have her stripped naked on the counter, but the sound of the kids coming down the hall has me setting the table instead.

It seems like the last part of the day goes by the quickest. All day long I watch the clock, waiting for closing time so I can spend the rest of the evening with my family, but when I get home, time flies away from me.

We have dinner, and after I help Brooklyn clean up, I chase after the kids. They scream and laugh as we play hide-and-seek, laser tag, and wrestle around. While Brook gives L.J. a bath, I have a tea party with my princess and her dolls. Never did I think that I would be sitting at a mini table with a pink boa wrapped around my neck, getting yelled at by a four-year-old about keeping my pinky up. But anything is better than having to ride on that tiny rocking horse again. Just thinking about how Brooklyn walked in to see my big frame on that tiny pink horse still cracks me up. My knees were damn near touching my chin while I rocked away on that thing.

L.J. comes running into the room, and he takes the teacup from my hand. "Okay, enough of this girlie stuff. It's time to play a man's game."

"Hey!" Jack yells.

I can't help but laugh. "All right, we'll go play cars while your sister gets her bath, and then it's time to settle down for a bedtime story."

Another hour later, the kids have had their bath, story, and bedtime snack. I get them all tucked in and walk into the bedroom to find Brooklyn sitting on the bed. She's wearing her sexy-as-hell reading glasses low on her nose as she reads over some documents. She's stripped free of her jeans, leaving her in only a pair of white lacy panties and one of my navy button-up shirts. Her long legs are outstretched, crossed at the ankles, teasing me.

She looks up. "Are they asleep?"

I smile and nod before crawling up the foot of the bed. My lips find the soft skin of her calf, and they make their way higher.

She giggles before tossing the papers to the side. "Don't you ever get enough? We just made love in the shower this morning."

I still have clothes on, but that doesn't stop my hips from moving against her hot center.

"What can I say? You're beautiful and smart, and I can't keep my hands off of you." I nuzzle into the crook of her neck.

"I swear, every time I start to get some actual work done, you come in here and – ohh." Her sentence comes to a stop when I slide my finger into the side of her panties.

I take my time teasing her and shove my jeans below my hips, but when I can no longer hold off, I thrust deep inside. She's hot, wet, and tight around me. I lose myself in her like I do every time we make love. I'd happily stay here forever if I could.

We don't part until several hours later, opting to go again and again.

My body is totally spent from the long day and the hours we gave to each other. My mind is completely still. My eyes have just closed when the sound of the phone on the bedside table rings loudly, cutting through the darkness and jolting me fully awake.

I rush to answer it before it wakes anyone up. "Hello?"

"John? It's Zoe," I make out through her sobs.

I sit up straight. "Zoe? What's the matter? Why are you crying?" I ask in a panic.

"It's Jake. He's gone."

"I'll be right there." I hang up the phone and shoot out of bed.

"What's going on?" Brook asks, sitting up in bed and watching me rush around the room for my clothes.

"That was Zoe on the phone. Something is wrong. I have to go over there."

She stands up suddenly. "Do I need to call Dad and have him sit with the kids so I can go with you?"

I walk over to where she is standing and press a kiss to her lips. "We don't have time. Go back to sleep. I'll be back as soon as possible."

I rush out of the house and down the road to Jake's. Zoe is standing in the open doorway as I'm walking up. Her T-shirt is stretching over her big pregnant belly, and she's trying to pull her robe tighter around herself. Her tears have dried, leaving a trail of mascara down her cheeks.

I walk in, and she closes the door behind me. "What's going on? Where is Jake?"

She slowly walks into the living room, falling down on the couch. "I don't know. He left this afternoon to deliver a car. He should have been back hours ago. He's not answering his phone, and the location on his phone is turned off. I'm worried. He wouldn't just not come home like this, John."

I nod as I sit down, elbows resting on my knees. "I know he wouldn't. Do you know who he was delivering the car to or their address?"

She shakes her head no with big tears running down her face again. "No, he didn't say. We were going to fry some fish for dinner. We made plans. I know he would be in a hurry to get home. Something has happened. I just know it."

I take her hands in mine. "I'm sure everything is okay. Calm down. He probably broke down on the side of the road or got a flat tire or something. How did he plan on getting back home? Was he going to get a ride back or what?"

"He didn't say, but I looked out the window just as he was pulling out and he had his bike loaded up. I'm guessing to get back home."

"He had his bike?" I ask, suddenly having my first clue.

"Yeah. Why?"

"Because all our bikes have trackers on them. If he took his bike, I can find it. I need to use your computer."

CHAPTER TWO

Jake

"Ah, my head." I try to lift my hands to rub it, but they are tied together behind me. Opening my eyes in the darkness, I can make out two men in the front seat. The radio is blaring, so I don't think they've heard me wake up. The leather of the seat is warm beneath my cheek. I draw my legs up only to find that they are bound together by rope like my hands. *What the hell? Who did I piss off?* My mind races to come up with someone.

The darkly tinted windows prevent me from seeing outside to figure out where I am. The way the vehicle is jostling around, I think we are off-road. The only light I see is coming from the dashboard and the blue hue of a cell phone that the man in the front seat is scrolling through.

I'm totally blank. The only person I ever piss off is John. The leather creaks as I attempt to sit and the passenger with the phone spins around with a gun pointed against my forehead.

"Stay the fuck down," he snarls.

"Where are you taking me?"

"You'll find out soon enough."

"I think you have the wrong person." That's it, they must have been after Glenn.

He chuckles. "Nope. You, Jake Remington, have a bounty on your head."

"Who would pay money for me? I'm a nobody, a hardworking man that keeps to himself."

"Obviously you have friends in low places, or I wouldn't be half a million dollars richer for taking your sorry ass to my boss."

"Who's your boss?"

"I'm done talking to you." He rears back, and I feel the cold metal of the gun on the side of my head.

"Damn my head hurts." My hands and feet are free this time, but I open my eyes to darkness again. My body is stiff, and my head hurts as I get off the bare concrete floor and feel my way around. There is a glimmer of light shining through a high rectangular-shaped window near the ceiling of the room. From what I can tell, I'm in a basement. It's hot and has a moldy smell permeating the room. My hands trail the empty walls as I keep feeling around; there is a metal door with a sliding latch on it and bars. A makeshift prison. I yank hard at the door, but it won't budge.

"Hello!" I yell. "Is anyone out there?" I start to panic in the small, dark confines. Running my hands down the pockets of my jeans, my phone is gone. I push the button on the side of my watch to give me a smidge of light. It doesn't help much because the walls look as black as night.

I take both hands and rattle the bars as hard as I can until my hands ache from squeezing them so tightly. The basement is so hot, sweat is beading down my face, and my T-shirt is damp. "Let me out of here!" I pound with my fists this time.

A thin beam of light comes from under a door above me, allowing me to make out a set of stairs confirming my thoughts about it being a basement. When the door opens, I see the silhouette of a man the size of a gorilla. The floor creaks, and I hear the tug of a chain and light fills the room.

"Get on your knees." It's the same voice from the car.

I slide to my knees and place my hands behind my head. "What do you want from me?"

"I don't want anything other than for you to quit making so much damn noise. You're making my fucking head throb," he growls as he comes further down the stairs.

"Your head throbs? Mine hurts because you keep hitting me," I bark back and rub the lump on the side of my head.

"If you don't shut up, I'll hit you again." He shows me his gun as it clangs up against the metal bars of my prison.

"Bossman said to drug him to keep him quiet." An even larger hulk of a man comes down the stairs holding a vial and a needle.

"I don't understand what's going on. Who is your bossman?"

"Someone that hates your brother and needs something from that pretty little wife of his."

"John? This is about John? Man, whatever he's done in the past, he's a changed man. And, Brooklyn is living a quiet life now. What could someone want from her?"

"Given a minute, I'd take her sexy body, but bossman wants that clever brain of hers." He laughs.

I can feel my blood start to boil and my protectiveness for her takes over. "Stay away from them, and whatever information you want from me, I won't tell you anything," I seethe. I don't know anything, but even if I did, I'd never tell them.

He pulls a key out of his black pants and unlocks the latch, pointing his gun at me again. He opens the door and steps inside with his bulky friend. I take a step back.

"Good thing all you have to do is shut up and not get on my nerves."

I'm the pawn. They're going to use me to get what they want from Brooklyn. I'm not going to let them drug me without a fight. I casually glance down and then come up swinging. I get one punch in and brace my hand over his that is holding the gun. A shot fires, ricocheting on the concrete walls. It bounces off, nearly missing me and hitting my captor in the thigh.

He crumbles to the floor with his gun still grasped in his hand, hitting his partner as he stumbles backward, knocking him off balance. It gives me the split second I need to move by them and run up the stairs.

My feet barely tap each stair as I run and open the door they came through. It opens up into a narrow kitchen. Quickly shutting it, I lock the door behind me and grab a knife left sitting on the counter beside a half-eaten sandwich. I make a quick sweep of the small house, looking for a phone, but only find a flashlight. I open the front door that empties onto white gravel. Swinging the light out, all I can see is land and the dark SUV.

I hear the locked door shake, followed by pounding and the grumble of a voice. I run to the SUV, hoping like hell it's unlocked. I don't need the keys to start it. I've hot-wired many cars before.

"Shit!" It's locked. I look around for anything I can use to break the window. As I scan the area, I realize I was wrong about it being a basement that I was held in. It's a container home with a bunker almost completely buried under the ground. Only three feet are above the earth with the thin window showing. The land around the house is barren other than the gravel. There is a steel perimeter fence around the property with a gated entrance.

The front door comes barreling open followed by the sound of a gun being shot. I turn off the flashlight and head for the fence. As I start to climb the eight-foot wall, my foot gets caught in one of the rungs. I yank my foot hard, but it won't come out. I hang tight with one hand and reach down and unlace my boot. I'm able to slip my foot out and keep climbing. Once I'm over the fence, I take off running in the darkness, having no idea where I am.

All I know is that I'm in an open field with nowhere to hide. Car lights flash from behind me, allowing me to see a line of trees out in the distance. If I can make it there, I might be able to find a place to hide. I pick up my stride and feel something dig into my socked foot, but I keep running, never slowing my pace. The SUV roars behind me just as I make it into the trees. Dust flies up as he slams on the brakes and then gunfire starts. The bullet hits the tree next to me, sending bark flying and scraping the side of my face.

I take off, going further into the wooded area until the shots ringing out are far enough behind me. I stop to catch my breath and to listen to the sounds around me. I can hear the sound of a river rushing over a waterfall. The moon is peeking out enough to light my way, and I start to walk in the direction of the flowing water. A flood of warmth beneath my foot has me stopping in my tracks. I look down to see that blood has soaked through my sock and I'm leaving a trail of bloody footprints behind me. I need to make it to the water, so they can't follow me. I take off in a run, despite the pain now searing through my foot.

I'm slowed down by having to climb down several big, slippery rocks. My fingers dig into the crevices, holding on for dear life. Once I clear them, I get into the water, and I take off running again and come to a jarring halt on the edge of the waterfall. I have to use my arms for balance to keep from falling downward.

I start to take off in the other direction and hear a baritone voice. A beam of light shines in my eyes. "Don't make me kill you," the hulk of a man says, pointing his gun at me.

I raise my hands in the air and take a step backward.

He leans his head to the side, cracking his neck. "You aren't worth anything to me dead."

I turn my head to the side, looking down behind me.

"Don't even think about it. You'll never survive the fall," he says as he sloshes closer in the water.

My mind flashes to Zoe and my unborn baby. I have to make it home to them to keep them safe. If I die, they might take them for whatever leverage it is that they need, but I refuse to be held captive. John lived like that for two years and barely survived. I won't do it, and I won't be used to get whatever they need from Brooklyn.

The cock of his gun echoes in my ear as I make the split decision to jump. I fall as if in slow motion. I can see the water below me lined with jagged rocks and whitewater out in front of me. Zoe's beautiful face flashes in front of me again. She pushes a blonde strand of hair out of her face, showing her silver-blue eyes. She's talking, but no sound is passing her lips. I can make out the words I love you as I crash into the water.

I'm pulled so far under and weighted down by clothes that I gasp for breath the second I come out of the water, only to be pulled under again. My left side crashes into to a rock, and I'm pushed into the white rapids from the impact. I gasp for air every time I can get my head above water. I draw my feet up and ride with the flow taking me further downstream. Once I'm able to get my feet on the ground, I stand and make my way to the muddy shoreline. I delve my hands into the mud and cover my face and white T-shirt. I take off in a run again for what seems like miles of rocky land. When I come to another ledge, I'm looking out over the Pacific Ocean.

"I'm on a fucking island." There has to be a bridge somewhere for them to have their car. Even if I found it, I'm sure that is the first place they'll be guarding. "Damn it." *What would John do?* I run my hand through my wet hair and wince when I touch the lump on my head.

I sit on the rocky ledge to look at my throbbing foot. Pulling my soaked sock off, I see a jagged cut about two inches long in my heel. Blood and water are pouring out of it. I hold pressure until it subsides. Then I make a makeshift bandage by tying my sock around it, hoping to keep it from bleeding again.

I stand back up and dig the flashlight out of my wet jeans. I click the button, but it doesn't come on. I slap it with my hand a few times, but it still doesn't work. I need to find shelter until the sun starts to come up, then I will have a better idea of how to get off this island and call for help. The only thing I see is one lone tree standing on the edge of the mountainous ledge.

I hobble my way over to it, careful not to put my heel on the ground so my wound doesn't reopen. I climb the monstrous tree, snapping small twigs on my way up. The canopy is so big that I won't be seen from any distance.

I wedge myself in between two branches and make myself as comfortable as possible with the thick bark grinding into my back.

I slow my breath and racing heart only for my mind to settle on my family again. What the hell could they possibly want from Brooklyn? I know she is still doing some research for cures, but she's been good about keeping it all quiet. She doesn't even have her lab registered anywhere. Who could be after her? Miles is dead, and all his men landed in jail. Maybe it has something to do with Matthew. He's retired, but still has plenty of power and I'm sure enemies.

Right now I need to focus on getting out of here and getting back to my family. The safety I've felt for the last four years is now gone. The fear for Zoe and the baby is real. How did John survive all those years not knowing if he'd ever get back to them?

I rest my head back on the tree and gaze out into the moonlit ocean until my eyes grow too heavy to keep them open.

CHAPTER THREE

John

I pull up the GPS on Jake's bike and find it a few towns over. No way he shouldn't be back by now. If he took the freeway, and knowing Jake I'm sure he did, the journey shouldn't take more than a couple of hours each way.

"I found it." I push away from the desk and rush toward the door with Zoe chasing after me as quickly as she can with her big pregnant belly.

"What are you going to do? Should I call the police?" she asks, standing by the open front door.

I turn around when I'm halfway to my bike. "Not yet. I need to figure out what it is we're dealing with here." I walk back up to her. "I know you don't know much about what I did before, but if anyone can find him, it's me. Trust me. Okay?"

She nods as a shuddering breath leaves her mouth. "Jake told me about you being held captive and escaping. I know you can do it. But please, John, be careful. Me and Brooklyn, we need our men."

"Go inside and try to relax. I'll let you know as soon as I find out what's happened to him."

I turn and jump on my bike, driving as quickly as I can. I need a few things if I'm going to go looking for Jake. There's no telling what I could be walking in on.

I go to my shop first and grab a couple of guns and some ammo. I tuck one gun into my boot and the other in the waistband of my jeans. I also grab my knife, placing it in the other boot.

I rush to the house to let Brooklyn know what is going on. I expect to find her in bed, fast asleep, but she's up pacing the bedroom floor. The second I walk in, she spins around to face me.

"What's going on, John? Is it starting again?"

I rush to the closet and get my leather coat. I walk back out, and the fear in her eyes breaks my heart. "Jake's missing."

"Missing? What do you mean he's missing?"

I shrug. "Zoe said he left this afternoon to deliver a car, and he hasn't come home. He's not answering his phone either. I tracked his bike, so I'm going to go check it out."

"Let me go with you!" She rushes past me, walking into the closet for some clothes.

I spin around quickly. "No! I'm not bringing you in on this. We have no idea what's going on. I want you here and safe."

She turns to me, determination radiating from her eyes. "If you think that I'm letting you walk out of here alone, you're crazy. The last time I left you, you were gone for two years."

I close the distance between us. "This isn't like it was before. We have two kids now, and they need you. We can't go off chasing the bad guys. If something happens..." My sentence breaks off. "They can't lose the both of us."

I can tell she feels defeated when she plops down on the bed.

"I promise —" My sentence is cut off when the phone rings.

We both turn to look at her ringing cell phone without moving. It's almost like we're afraid to answer it.

Suddenly, time kicks back in, and we both move toward it. She picks it up and looks at the screen. "It's a call through FaceTime, but I don't recognize the number."

"Give it to me," I say, reaching for the phone. She hands it over, and I press Accept.

The line clicks and then I'm looking at Knox, the man that put the hit out on Brooklyn all those years ago, the man that brought us together. "John, how you been doing?" His voice is raspy, and his short hair all gray now. The wrinkles on his face are deeper, aging him ten years.

"A lot better than you by the looks of it," I reply, seeing the bars of his jail cell behind him.

He lets out a deep laugh. "Always with the jokes, John. You haven't changed a bit. That's what I've been counting on."

I shake my head. "I don't know what you want, but you can forget it."

I'm about to hit the End button, but he stops me by saying, "I trust you've had the time needed to discover Jake's disappearance."

I freeze. "You're behind that?" My blood starts to boil beneath my skin. "Where is he, you son of a bitch?"

He *tsk's* me. "If you ever want to see him again, I'd try showing a little respect to your elders, boy."

I take a deep breath to cool off. Pissing him off will only make it worse. "What do you want?"

He leans back in his seat. "What everyone wants, really." He offers a wicked smile. "Freedom, John. I want my freedom, and you're going to give it to me."

I laugh as I run my hand through my hair. "Are you fucking kidding me? You want me to break you out of prison?"

He nods. "It's a minimum-security prison. If anyone can do it, it's you."

"Minimum security? I thought you were locked up in a dark hole somewhere."

He laughs. "I was moved to reward my good behavior, not to mention the overpopulation problem at max. So what do you say, John? Are you in, or are you going to kiss that twin brother of yours goodbye?"

I rub my forehead, hoping to ease away the stress, but it does no good. My stomach rolls at the thought of doing anything that he wants. But, he's ruthless, and he will kill Jake. There is no doubt in my mind about it. I look at the screen. "I'll do it."

"What? John, no!" Brooklyn screams from my side.

"Oh, good. Just the woman I was wanting to speak to," Knox says after he hears Brooklyn's voice.

"She's not speaking to you," I tell him with a sharp edge to my voice.

"Well she's going to have to because this next part involves her."

She moves to my side as we both look at the man on the phone. I can see the fear building behind Brooklyn's eyes as she bites the inside of her cheek.

"I need the cure, Brooklyn."

I glance over at her, and she quickly looks at me before she takes the phone from my hand. "What cure? I don't have a cure. The cure for cancer is out, despite you wanting to kill me for it!"

He shakes his head. "Not that one. The cure for Alzheimer's."

The fear that was chiseled in her eyes moments ago has turned to panic. I can see it written all over Brooklyn's face.

"I don't have the cure. I haven't been able to figure it out yet. And how the hell do you know what I've been working on?"

"I have my ways of getting information. What I know doesn't matter. You better figure it out, or you'll never see Jake again. I'd hate to have to add Zoe and that unborn child to the list."

"You better not lay a finger on her, you slimy bastard," Brooklyn seethes.

"Do your job and find the cure. All of their lives depend on it. Oh, and John, the sooner, the better. The food here is terrible." With that, he hangs up the call.

Brooklyn lets the phone slip from her fingers. It goes crashing to the floor. "John, you can't do this."

I pull her against me. "I have to. I have to save my brother. He's done so much for me. I can't let anything happen to him."

"My father is no longer in the presidency. If you get caught, you'll be in prison right along with him." She looks up at me with wide eyes that are back to being full of fear, but now worry has crept into the lines of her face.

"Then we'll have to make sure I don't get caught." I press a kiss to her lips and pull away, heading for the door.

"Where are you going?"

My hand is on the doorknob, but I stop and turn back to look at her. "I have to do some recon on his prison. Find out how things work there. And you, you need to get busy too." I turn and head for my office.

Since the bastard was kind enough to leave out what prison he's in, it takes me a good hour of hacking and following paper trails to find out where he is now. I come upon a transfer document that states he was moved to a minimum-security prison in Arizona. I look the prison up to get a clear picture of the layout. The building is in the shape of a rectangle, with a twelve-foot chain-link fence surrounding it. The courtyard is in the opening in the center of the building, meaning the prisoners don't even have access to the fence. The only way I'm going to get him out of there is getting on the inside.

Trapped inside a prison is not the place I want to be.

"Fuck," I yell as I toss the pen I was clicking across the room.

Brooklyn walks in with a hot cup of coffee. She places it in front of me while perching on the edge of the desk. "Not having any luck?"

I spin around to face her while rubbing my hands over my face. "I don't know how in the hell I'm going to pull this off."

She stands and moves around me, starting to knead her fingers into my shoulders. "You've done some amazing things, John. If anyone can figure it out, it's you. Plus, it's not like you have to find a cure for a disease that's been plaguing people since the beginning of time."

I turn my chair and pull her down onto my lap. "We're fucked."

"Yep," she agrees with a nod.

CHAPTER FOUR

Jake

The sunrise over the ocean isn't its normal orange and pink but the pale gray color of a worn-out dime, and there is a fine mist of rain starting to fall. I stretch my aching body from the position I've held all night. It's the first time in a long time that I've feared facing the day. Zoe must be frantic by now with worry. Surely she's called John, and he's already looking for me. He knows he can track me by my motorcycle. That will at least lead him to Glenn's house. I'm not sure what he will find from there.

Zoe is a strong, independent woman, but I worry about her being so upset and pregnant. The stress on her and the baby can't be good. I rub my hand over my heart as I think about the two of them. I'll never forget the day I first laid on eyes on her. I met her through Brooklyn. She answered an ad that Brooklyn put online for an assistant. She had great research and computer skills, so Brooklyn hired Zoe on the spot. The first time she introduced us, I fell hard.

Her silver eyes locked on mine. "It's nice to meet you, Jake." Her delicate hand with perfectly manicured nails landed in my outstretched hand.

What I wouldn't give to have her fingernails leave an impression on my back. I released her hand. "You do research. Do you know what my shirt is made of?"

She looked at me confusedly, and I saw Brooklyn roll her eyes. "Cotton," she answered.

"Boyfriend material," I said, grinning at her. Brooklyn snorted in laughter.

It took a minute, but Zoe finally laughed. "Oh, I get it."

"I have plenty more. Your lips look lonely...would they like to meet mine? Or better yet, did you have Lucky Charms for breakfast? Because you look magically delicious."

She smiled a beautiful smile and Brooklyn walked over and yanked my ear, pulling me to the side. "Where the hell did you get those stupid pickup lines? You are going to scare her off. How can two brothers be so different? She let go of my ear and crossed her arms over her chest.

"I Googled them. How else do you think I could be so charming? I'll teach John a few for you since you seemed to like them so much."

Zoe laughed from behind her. "It's okay. What he lacks in charm, he makes up for in his good looks." She winked at Brooklyn.

I was a goner; hook, line, and sinker.

God, we've had some good times since then. When she told me she was pregnant, I wanted to get married right away, but she wanted to wait until after the baby was born. Right now, I wish I would have convinced her to marry me on the spot. I didn't see the point in waiting. She's the love of my life, and nothing is ever going to change that. She didn't want to walk down the aisle with a big belly. She wants a grand wedding with her entire family that consists of three brothers and two sisters. None of which live in Hawaii. I would give her the world if that's what she wants. I need to make my way back to her.

I stand on a limb, looking to see if there is anyone around. The coast is clear, so I climb down out of the tree, cautious of my foot. The rain is starting to fall harder and the mud I rubbed on my face is dripping down my skin, making me itch.

I'm a sitting duck out here in the open, so I make my way back to the woods. There is a clay path that runs alongside the outside of the woods. I couldn't see it last night, and I'm not sure I want to follow it now, but it will probably lead me back to the house. If I see anyone coming, I'm close enough to run into the trees. The clouds rolling in are thick, and I can only see a few hundred feet in front of me.

The rain is coming down in pelts and slowing me down. I follow the path down a steep slope, and I can hear voices. I'm no longer next to trees, but large rocks. I dart behind one and listen to which direction the voices are coming from. I hear two men talking to the left of me. The rocks beneath their feet crunch as they move toward me.

"No, I didn't tell him that he escaped. We would lose the money he's paying us, and he might have us killed," one of them says.

"He's in prison. I don't think he can kill us."

"You're an idiot. He puts contracts out on people for a living. I don't think it would be difficult for him to have us taken out."

I hold my breath as they walk by, not wanting to make the least little bit of noise. Once they are far enough past me, I take in a breath. Their boss must be Knox. What the hell does he want with Brooklyn? Maybe it's another ploy to get his revenge on John. I have to find a way to warn him.

I follow the path, and it leads me exactly where I thought it would, back to the house. The SUV is still parked out front, but now there is another gray pickup truck parked beside it. I don't see any movement coming from the house, so I make my way to the truck and duck down, waiting to see if I've been seen. I reach up to the passenger side door of the truck, and it's unlocked. I climb inside and keep low. I find the wires that I need and start the engine. I quickly get behind the wheel and throw the truck in reverse. As I peel out of the driveway, the front door flies open, and two men come out shooting. I hear the splinter of the bullet impact the truck. I turn the wheel sharp and head for the closed gate. I give it gas and hit the gate, throwing it into the air and over the top of the truck. I turn on the wipers so I can see the road in front of me. In the rearview mirror, the SUV is moving in behind me.

I have no idea where I am or where the road leads. I can only hope it takes me off the island. I hold on for dear life as the truck bounces over potholes and large rocks. The back window shatters as bullets comes flying through it. I accelerate again but hear the loud *pop* of one of the tires then the sound of another one right behind it. I lose control and careen off into a ditch and smack hard against a tree. The airbag dislodges, smacking me right in the face, dazing me. I get the door open and fall out onto the ground. I scramble trying to get up but feel the jab of a needle in the side of my neck.

"God, you're beautiful in the morning." I kissed Zoe's shoulder as she stretched awake.

"You need glasses." She laughed.

I rolled on top of her, pinning her to the bed. "I'm the luckiest man alive," I said, trailing kisses down her long slender neck, and she wiggled underneath me.

"Right now, I'd say I'm pretty lucky." Her hands squeezed my ass, pushing my hard cock into her core. I tweaked her nipple; she jolted upward, and I pressed down, holding her in place. "Sit still so I can worship your body." I moved downward, nipping as I go to her taut belly.

"Jake, I have to tell you something. I wanted to tell you last night, but you were out so late working in the garage, I fell asleep before you got home." Her hands toyed with my hair.

"Whatever it is, I think it can wait. I want to make it up to you for being out so late last night."

She tugged at my hair. "I don't want to wait."

"Now you have me worried." I climbed back up her body to look her in the eyes.

"We're pregnant."

A banging noise has me bolting up straight. I've moved so fast that a wave of nausea rolls over me. My head is spinning, and I'm in a cold sweat.

"Bossman says I can't kill you, so I need to feed you."

The big hulky man from before unlocks the latch and slides in a plate of food. "Don't try any shit or I'll drug you again," he says, locking my prison up tight.

I'm back where I started. How the hell am I going to get out of here again? I lie back down on the concrete floor and glance over at the plate of food. It's some kind of sandwich and an apple. Right now I'd give my left nut for a bottle of water. I'm so parched, and I think I have dried mud in my mouth.

My stomach finally quits rolling, and I decide I need to eat the food to keep up my strength so I can escape again. I swallow down the stale white bread and try to remember all the ways John told me he tried to escape. This place is completely empty, and there is nothing for me to use. I stare down at my one boot and remember him telling me that he used his shoestring to choke one of his captors. I unlace my black boot and pull the string out, throwing my boot off. He also told me that he used a guard's key to jab into his jugular to kill him. That will be my plan next time one of them comes into my jail. I'll steal their weapon and take the rest of them out. For now, all I can do is sit and wait.

The time rolls by so slowly. Every now and then I hear voices. They are passing the time watching television as I sit down here plotting my escape. I don't want to kill them, but if it's my only hope to get out of here, I will. It would be self-defense; it's the only way I could do it. God knows I love my brother, but I don't know how he was a hitman. He had his reasons, but I'm glad I was never put in his shoes. I don't think I could have walked in them. I would kill to save Zoe, Brooklyn, the kids, and even for John, so *my life* shouldn't be any different.

The room is getting dark again as night falls. The drugs have finally cleared my aching head. I stand and rattle my cage to get their attention. "I need some water," I yell.

The door comes open, and a man I've never seen before is at the top of the stairs. "What?" he growls.

"I need some water and to use the bathroom."

He slams the door and returns in a few minutes with a bottle of water in one hand and a bucket in the other. Another man follows him downstairs with a gun pointed at me. "No escaping for you this time," he says. "Back up against the wall."

I do as he says. I won't be able to follow through with my plan this time, but there will be a moment when one of them comes down here alone, and then I'll put my plan into action.

He opens the door far enough to shove the bucket and the bottle of water through. "That's the only bathroom you are getting." He laughs. He locks it back up and then stomps up the stairs, slamming the door behind them.

I relieve myself and gulp down the water. It barely touches the dryness of my mouth. I wish my throat was as wet as my clothes. I might as well get some sleep and try again tomorrow. I curl up into a ball and close my eyes, but all I see is Zoe's face. The time we've shared together plays over and over in my mind like a movie. Snapshots of us down by the ocean, game night with John and Brooklyn, cooking out in the backyard. Making love by the star-filled night out on our back porch. Tears flood my eyes when I think about not seeing her again or never experiencing the birth of our child. A blonde-haired little girl that looks just like her mother.

I know John and Brooklyn would step in to help raise the baby, but damn it, I want to be the one that sees her grow into a beautiful young lady. I want every moment with her, including the tea parties and playing with her princess dolls. I'm not too proud. I want to be a good father and husband. I don't want her raised by another man. And, God forbid, the thought of Zoe being with another man sets me on fire. I sit up, gasping for air. I've got to calm down, or I won't make it out of here. I take in some slow, deep breaths, calming my nerves. Lying back on the hard floor, I lay still in the darkness and will myself to sleep.

CHAPTER FIVE
John

I've been in front of the computer all night; I'm no closer to finding a way to get Knox out without getting myself caught in the process. I'd be the first person to go to prison for breaking *into* a prison.

Brooklyn was beside me most of the night with file folders and papers galore. She finally fell asleep on the couch next to my desk around four a.m. She didn't even budge when I removed her reading glasses that had slipped down her nose and were covering her mouth. Little puffs of air fogged the lenses.

It's now going on seven, and the kids are beginning to stir. I push away from my desk to get them up so Brooklyn can sleep a little longer, but the wheels rolling across the hardwood floor jolt her awake. "I'm working," she mumbles as she sits up and licks her lips while wiping the sleep from her eyes.

I stand with a laugh and kiss her on the head. "Why don't you go to bed for a few hours? I can handle the kids."

"No way can I sleep until I have this figured out. I owe Jake so much. I have to work," she argues, shaking her head vigorously.

I stop at the open door. "I can't make you sleep, but I can make you take a break. Neither of us are going to figure this out if we're going crazy. Let's take an hour or so, eat some breakfast with the kids, and then we'll get the nanny to take them out for the day so we can get back to work. Deal?"

"All right. You get the kids up and dressed, and I'll start on breakfast."

Brooklyn heads downstairs for the kitchen, and I stop in L.J.'s room first. He's up and playing with his cars on the floor.

"Good morning, buddy," I say on my way to his dresser to find him some clothes.

"Morning, Dad!" he replies cheerfully.

I dig his clothes out of the drawer and toss them to him. "Put those on and be in the kitchen in five. Got it?"

"Yep!" He's always so happy in the mornings. It's exhausting.

I walk into Jack's room, and she's tossing and turning in bed. She's the one that likes her sleep. Her little body is saying it's time to wake up, but she's not having it. She will toss and turn until she wills herself back to sleep.

"Come on, princess. Let's get up and get some break-fast in that tummy." I dig around for her clothes.

"No, I sleepy," she mumbles.

I fall to my knees beside her toddler bed and pull the blanket away from her face. "If you get up and get dressed, I promise to take you out to the range soon and let you shoot." She takes after me more than I'm prepared for. She loves getting to shoot, and for a four-year-old, she has damn good aim. I'll keep her using the BB gun until she's a little older though.

"Yay!" she cheers as she pops up, jumping up and down on her little bed.

I quickly tug a pink shirt over her head and pair it with leggings. "All right, go potty and get down to the kitchen. Okay? No dolls this morning. We don't have time."

"Okay, Daddy," she says as she twists a lock of hair at the crown of her head.

I wander down into the kitchen and find Brooklyn behind the stove. She's moving like a sloth, but I can't blame her. We've been backed into a corner and have no choice but to fight our way out. We're both tired and stressed.

"Need help with anything?" I ask as I pour the kids some milk and place their cups on the table.

"I'd love another cup of coffee. Something tells me I'm going to need it." She polishes off the last sip from her mug and hands it to me.

I get to work pouring us both, what must be, our twentieth cup of coffee. "Where is your dad this morning? He coming for breakfast?"

"No, he left yesterday morning for some golf tournament. He won't be back until this weekend. Have you filled Zoe in on what we found out last night?"

I shake my head before taking a sip. "No. I'll give her a call after breakfast. I'm sure she's tired and probably still sleeping since she was up late last night."

Both kids come running down the stairs at the same time. They're both jumping up and down at my feet, wanting to play.

I reach down and pick up L.J. "We'll have to play later, buddy. It's time to eat." I step around Jack and place L.J. in his chair at the table.

I turn around to pick Jack up, but she jumps up and hits me right in the balls. She's the perfect height and drills me there almost every day. I freeze and hold my breath, trying to power through.

Brooklyn turns around, sees my face, and knows exactly what happened. She laughs out loud. It's the first sign of something other than worry I've seen on her face since before we went to bed last night.

"I'm glad you're done having children because my boys aren't going to survive this one," I say, referring to Jack. I pick her up and put her down in the chair.

"Jack, honey, I told you that you're too strong for Daddy. You have to be careful so you don't hurt him."

She smiles and nods before sticking out her tongue at L.J.

L.J. doesn't like to be shown up. He crosses his arms over his chest. "She's not stronger than Dad. She just hit him in the balls!"

I bust out laughing, but Brooklyn gives me the death glare. "We don't say that, buddy," I tell him with the most serious tone I can muster, while a smile continues to play on my lips.

Brooklyn places the kids' plates in front of them, and I take ours and set them down on the table. We all sit to eat together. The kids are arguing back and forth about whatever it is they're talking about, but Brook is quiet as she's chewing slowly. I can tell she's worried when all she does is pick at her food.

"We'll figure this out, I promise." I reach over and place my hand on her free one.

Her eyes meet mine, and for the first time since we've been together, I can tell she doesn't believe me.

"Easy for you to say. You're not the one that has to discover an impossible cure. You know I've been working on this for years. How am I supposed to come up with the answer like that?" She snaps her fingers.

"I don't know, but if anyone can —"

"I know, I know," she interrupts me. "You have way too much confidence in my abilities."

We finish up breakfast, and the kids run off to play. "Why don't you call the nanny and I'll call Zoe," I tell her as we're cleaning up the kitchen.

She dries her hands and picks up her cell phone to make the call. I'm digging through my jeans pocket to call Zoe when I hear the front door slam shut. I turn around to see Zoe barreling toward me.

"I'm calling the police. He's been gone too long. Something is wrong! I've been up all night pacing the floor, waiting for you to call me!"

I place my hands on her shoulders. "Calm down, Zoe. Please, sit down." I back up her a few steps, and she sits down in the kitchen chair. "Do you want some tea or coffee?"

She reaches over and snags a piece of bacon from the center of the table. "No, but some chocolate milk would be amazing. Can I eat the rest of this?" She points to the leftover eggs, toast, and bacon on the table.

"Help yourself," I say as I spin around to pour her a glass of chocolate milk. If food keeps her calm, I'll make her a feast.

Brooklyn hangs up the phone and sits next to Zoe. "The nanny will be here soon. Did you tell her yet?"

"Tell me what?" Zoe asks, crunching on a well-cooked piece of bacon.

I cross my arms over my chest and lean against the counter. "I got a call last night."

"From Jake? Is he okay? Why didn't he come home? And, why didn't you tell me last night?" she asks in a rush.

I hold up my hand. "Not from Jake. Jake is still missing, but I know who is behind his disappearance."

"Jake is being held for ransom." I run my hand through my hair, trying to keep myself calm so that maybe Zoe will calm down.

"Ransom? What do they want and who are they?" She's back to being frantic.

"The impossible," Brooklyn mumbles.

Zoe quickly turns to look at her, then she slowly looks at me.

I give Brooklyn an annoyed glance. I know she's stressed and tired, but she should be trying to keep Zoe calm.

"It's the same man that put a hit out on Brooklyn, but he doesn't want Jake dead. He's hired men to do his dirty work. He wants some help, and Brooklyn and I are more than capable of giving them what he wants. We just need a little time is all."

"So did you ever go and check out his bike? What if he's still there? And, what is it they want?"

"He's not," I reply. "As far as what he wants, he wants to be released from prison and for Brooklyn to cure him."

"But what if someone there saw something?" I see the rest of my answer finally register on her face. "Prison? What cure?"

I take a deep, calming breath. "If it makes you feel any better, I'll go by today and check it out, but I doubt that I'll find anything. The man that I used to work for wants his freedom."

"Yeah, he wants a cure that's not been found yet," Brooklyn adds, and I scowl at her.

Zoe begins to cry while rubbing her swollen belly. I kneel down in front of her. "Jake will be fine. They won't do anything to him because they need him for leverage. We'll get them what they want, and they will let him go. It's just going to take some time. Please have faith in us. We've taken on more than this before."

She sniffles and nods.

I stand and look at Brooklyn. "Can I talk to you in private for a minute?"

She nods and stands to follow me into the laundry room that's off of the kitchen.

"I'm going to go check out the location of the bike to make Zoe feel better."

"You won't find anything there, you said so yourself. Why waste the time?"

"Because it will ease Zoe's mind. She needs some peace. Plus, I don't have to be in front of a computer to put together a plan. Are you going to be okay while I'm gone?"

She pushes her red hair away from her face. "I'll be fine. I'm going to head to my office as soon as the kids are gone. Be careful." I reach out and grab the front of her shirt, pulling her closer. Her lips find mine, and her tongue dips inside.

I place my hand on either side of her face and kiss her deeply, wanting to assure her that we will make it through this. We have to. I will not let anything happen to my brother. He's already been through hell and back for me.

We pull away from one another, and I turn back toward the kitchen but pause. "I love you."

"I love you too. Say goodbye to the kids before you leave."

"I will. Try to get Zoe to go upstairs and lay down, would ya? The last thing she needs is exhaustion on top of all this stress. Jake will never forgive us if something happens to her or the baby because we were too busy to pay attention to her."

She nods as she takes my hand. "I will. Be careful."

It takes me a few hours to drive to where Jake's bike's GPS says it is. I pull into the parking lot of an apartment building. I park my truck and get out, walking through the lot, looking for his bike. I don't see it in between the cars, but I do see it loaded up in the back of an El Camino. I walk over to the vehicle and look it over for any signs of a struggle. It has a shiny new exterior with no scratch marks on it.

"Hey! Can I help you?" a man with dark hair asks as he comes running over to me.

"Yeah. I was wondering who owns this car."

"I do. Is there a problem?" he asks.

"That's my brother's bike, and he's missing. Can you tell me anything about that?" I casually place my hand on the handle of my gun in the back of my jeans.

"Oh, man. Jake's missing?"

I turn to face him. "You know him? Is this the car he delivered?"

"Yeah, he brought it up yesterday."

"What happened?" I can feel the tension coming off me in waves. If it wasn't for his sincere concern, I'd already have my finger wrapped around his throat for answers.

"I don't know." He rubs his head while thinking it over. "I came home to find him waiting on me. I got in the car and was checking it out. When I turned back to face him, Jake was out cold, lying on the ground." He takes a deep breath. "I jumped out of the car and ran over to him to check him out, and that's when I was hit over the head. When I came to, he was gone."

"And you didn't think to call the police?" I ask, not that they would've done a lot of good.

"I mean, it crossed my mind, but I'm an ex-con. I didn't want to be linked to that. I didn't see anything, and I have no idea what happened..."

Before he can process what I'm doing, I'm grabbing hold of him and throwing him up against the side of his car. "If I find out you're lying..."

He holds his hands up. "I'm not, man. I swear. Jake's my friend. I wouldn't ever be involved in something like that. I just got out of prison, and I'm not trying to go back."

I can see the fear in his eyes. I was a hitman. I'm good at reading people and this man, he didn't have anything to do with what happened to my brother.

I release him and pull a card out of my pocket. "If you hear anything, or think of anything, give me a call."

He takes the card from me. "I will. Please let me know if there is anything I can do."

I'm walking to my truck but turn back around. "Actually, there is." I move to the back of the vehicle and open the tailgate. "Give me a hand loading up his bike. No way am I leaving it here. It would be sold for parts."

CHAPTER SIX
Brooklyn

"I've been searching for the cure for Alzheimer's for years now. I don't know how he expects me to come up with one because he demands it," I grumble to myself as I put my white lab coat on. The nanny is watching the kids while Zoe tries to get a nap. Most of the time, I love coming to my lab and doing research, but under these circumstances, I don't want to be here. I sit down and push my reading glasses to the bridge of my nose.

"All the tests I've done, and I'm not even close," I continue to talk to myself. "Find the cure for Alzheimer's, Brooklyn—like it's as simple as baking cookies," I mock. "Mmmm...cookies, now that would give me some brain power." I rub my stomach as my mouth waters. "Focus, Brooklyn, get your mind off food for once."

I stand from the cold metal stool and flip the many labeled glass slides and place one under the microscope, staring at it like it's going to tell me its secrets. "Damn it, if I can't figure this out, we may never get Jake back." I can't lose him. He's the closest thing I have to a brother. He stood by me and helped me raise L.J. when John was held captive. God, I swear I thought all this was behind us. We had four blissful years, and now it's starting all over again. I don't like the thought of John being out there alone again, but he's right; I have to be here for our kids. Still, I want to be out there helping him.

Reaching over to the shelf, I turn on some music. It always helps settle my mind and gets me to focus. It's a soft melody that soothes me. I stretch my neck from side to side, relaxing the strain that has been building since Knox's phone call.

As I'm pulling out my latest journal of findings off the shelf, I hear the door open.

"Hey, Brooklyn," Zoe says with her hand splayed on her baby bump.

"I thought you were getting a nap?"

"I can't sleep knowing Jake is out there somewhere going through God knows what. He told me bits and pieces of what these people did to John." Her voice ends in a sob.

I get up and hug her to me. "John will find him. He's not going to let Jake suffer like he did. We didn't know John was alive or we would have fought for him a lot sooner. He knows how these men operate. He'll figure something out." I let go, and she wipes a tear from her cheek.

"I can't sit around here and do nothing."

"Then bring that brilliant mind of yours over here and help me solve the puzzle of Alzheimer's disease." I roll my comfortable desk chair in her direction.

"You and I have been researching this for months," she says as she sits.

"I know, but we are missing something. Let's go over the very basics of what we know." I start pacing the floor. "There are two abnormal structures when it comes down to damaging and killing nerve cells in our brains: plaques and tangles. We know that plaques are protein deposits that can build up in the space between the nerve cells, causing failure to communicate. The tangles are the twisted fibers of protein that block communication of the nerve cells. And, we know this is normal in aging, but an excessive amount of buildup of these two is what causes Alzheimer's. It's these nerve cells dying that cause memory loss and other symptoms."

Zoe is tapping her fingernails on the metal table as I continue my pacing. "We've tried a vaccine to get rid of the plaque. It failed. We've talked about coiling in the brain, and there are too many areas to have any real success. So, how do we break up the plaque and untangle the fibers at the same time?" I tap my fingers on my chin.

"What if we didn't have to do both?"

I stop pacing. "What do you mean?"

"If we could stop the production of plaque and remove it, the fibers would untangle themselves."

"We've tried a various mixture of drugs and nothing has worked." I sit on the edge of the table.

"When cardiologists remove plaque from the coronary arteries, they either stent through it, drill it, or suck it out. Or, a thoracic surgeon performs a bypass, creating a new passage for blood flow to feed the heart."

"We already know we can't stent it or bypass it." I blow a strand of hair out of my face and push my glasses back up.

"We can't suck it out either. Gah, this is getting us nowhere." She lays her head on the table.

"We don't have a choice. Knox will not stop until he has what he wants, so unless we can find where they are keeping Jake, we have to keep working on this." Her tears start to flow again, and she places her hands behind her back.

"Are you okay?" I point to her belly.

"My back has been bothering me since I got up this morning."

"Any contractions?"

"No, it's too soon. I'm not due for another six weeks."

"You know as well as I do that stress can bring on labor."

"I'm fine. I just had an ultrasound two days ago, and she's perfect. Those things are amazing now. They are so clear I can see that she has Jake's chin. The technology with ultrasound waves allows them to visualize all the major vessels in the body. They can see blood flowing through the brain, heart, and kidneys."

"Everything is good?"

"She's perfect. She just needs more time to grow." She rubs her belly again.

"I'm so happy for you and Jake. He's been through so much with his own cancer, losing his twin brother, and having to deal with me. He deserves a crown."

"I don't know how you survived all that you went through."

"I survived because of Jake and L.J. I wouldn't have made it without them."

"Jake says the same thing about you. He wouldn't have survived cancer without your cure. It's too bad the pharmaceutical companies tried to destroy you for such noble work. You could be doing so many amazing things, and you're here in this small lab that nobody knows about." She points around the room.

"I can't risk my family again. If I happen to find the cure for Alzheimer's, I was going to release it anonymously to one of my colleagues I worked with at a small research company."

"You wouldn't even take credit for finding the cure?"

"No. I don't want credit. I only want to cure a disease that leaves a person and their families shattered and heartbroken watching the person they love become someone else. It's a grueling disease, one that I wouldn't wish on anyone."

"Not even Knox?"

"Well, maybe him." I start pacing again, and Zoe stands with her hands on her lower back and starts stretching. "Maybe you should go see your doctor. You could be in the early stages of labor."

"I'm fine. We have too much work to do." Worry is etched on her face, and her silver-blue eyes look gray today. "Do you think he's okay?"

"I don't think they'll hurt him—he wants the cure too badly. If he kills him, he won't get what he wants. Besides, if Jake is anything like his brother, they need to fear him. He's probably plotting his escape as we speak." I laugh.

"I'm sure you're right. I just wish..."

"Wish what, Zoe?" I squat down in front of her.

"I wish I would've married him when he asked me to. It was silly of me to want to wait until the baby was born. I don't need an elaborate wedding. All I need is him." A tear falls.

"The Remington boys are hard to live with and without," I say, and she bursts out laughing through her tears. "They can be terribly sweet, pigheaded, charming, determined, and..." I continue.

"Controlling in the bedroom," she blurts out.

"Oh my God, it's not just John," I say, laughing.

"Nope. I think it must be an inherited trait." She giggles more.

"I let John think he's in control. He may be the head of this family, but I'm the neck."

"I've never thought of it that way. I like it!" Her face is back to glowing with our banter.

"Now that we know who is really in control, let's get back to our research."

"Before we do that, I downloaded the ultrasound. Would you like to see your beautiful niece?" She stands and heads to the computer.

"I would love to." I join her. She pulls the files up, and the baby's face appears. "She does have Jake's chin." She switches files to the entire body so that you can see every organ and the blood actually flowing.

"Does my sweet little niece have a name yet?"

"No, we can't agree on one." She closes the file and sits back down at the table and opens one of our many research books.

I keep an eye on her for any signs of early labor. As I'm watching her, an idea hits me. "Zoe. What if we've been going about this the wrong way?"

"What do you mean?"

"A vaccine will never work, and we can't go directly into the brain to cure it, but what if we used ultrasound waves to dissolve the plaque, which in return would straighten out the tangles with the plaque gone. By dissolving it with the waves, the plaque can't travel to other places in the body."

"Oh my God! That just might work!" She's up on her feet, reaching for the phone.

"Who are you calling?"

"I know a lab in California we can use to see if it will work."

"Wait, you aren't going anywhere, and I can't leave you here by yourself. I can get the equipment we need overnighted from my old company. Besides, I don't want anyone else knowing what we're doing. I can trust the people I worked with and developed the cure for cancer with."

She puts the phone down. "Okay. I'll work on getting the software we're going to need."

We both scramble. I make phone calls while she delves into the computer. This has to work. I don't know why I hadn't thought of it before. Seeing Zoe's ultrasound made things click. This has to work for Jake's sake. I know I told Zoe they wouldn't hurt him, but Knox is ruthless, and if he doesn't get what he wants, there is no telling what he'll do to Jake. My only hope is that he can find a way to escape if I can't make this all work out to cure the disease. It's a long shot, but it's the only one I have in keeping the Remington brothers out of trouble or worse, dead.

CHAPTER SEVEN

John

After Jake's bike is loaded up in the back of my truck, I hit the road in a hurry to get back home. I have too many things on my mind. I knew I wouldn't accomplish anything by coming here, but I did at least get Jake's bike. I feel like I'm working a cold case. In fact, the only useful piece of information I got by coming here was that I learned that there are traffic cameras in the area. I'm going to go home and hack into them, see if I can find anything that could help us out.

Jake being gone is eating at me. I can't stand that we've been brought back into this shit. And at a time when Zoe needs Jake the most. She's a good woman. She needs her soon-to-be husband, and that little girl she's carrying is going to be needing her daddy. I missed L.J. being born, and there's not a day that goes by that I don't regret it; I don't want him to know that same regret.

On the drive home, my mind drifts on its own to all the time we've spent together over the years. I start thinking about the first time I met Zoe.

I closed the shop up a little late and went straight home. Brooklyn called earlier, talking my ear off about Jake and her new assistant hitting it off. I pulled into the driveway and walked inside to find Brooklyn in the kitchen.

I wrapped my arms around her. "Hey."

She spun around and smacked a kiss against my lips. "Hi," she said cheerfully when she pulled away. Her dark eyes were bloodshot and glassy and her cheeks were a burning pink color. I knew that look well. She'd been drinking.

I laughed. "What's going on? Where are the kids?" I asked because we may have a glass of wine with dinner, but we didn't ever really drink with them home.

She rushed around the kitchen, pouring two more glasses of wine and taking two beers out of the fridge, handing me one. "They are staying the night with my dad. My assistant and your brother are flirting like fireworks are going off out there." She jumped up and down.

I laughed. "Are you sure? Jake's usually shy and awkward. If he thinks he's flirting, I'm sure he's just making an ass out of himself." I popped the top on my beer and took a long drink.

She nodded. "Oh, I'm sure. Zoe and I were working, and Jake stopped by. I noticed them checking one another out when they thought nobody was looking, and Jake kept giving her corny pickup lines, so I invited them both to stay for drinks and dinner. Get your brother's beer and follow me out back. We have fondue and a fire." She picked up both glasses of wine and rushed out the back door.

I grabbed Jake's beer and followed her. The second I walked out, I heard a woman laughing followed by Jake's deep chuckle. As I stepped closer, I watched as the woman latched onto Jake's bicep, slightly squeezing and rubbing before pulling away.

I almost stopped dead in my tracks. Way to go, Jake! Now I see why Brook was so excited.

I walked up to them and handed Jake his beer.

"Thanks, brother. Have you met Zoe yet?"

He tilted his beer up and took a swig. "I haven't had the pleasure yet." I held out my hand. "I'm John."

She placed her hand in mine. "Zoe." Her eyes bounced back and forth between Jake and me. "Wow, you two are twins? Why didn't you tell me that?" she asked Brooklyn.

Brook laughed; she'd had a little too much wine already. "I forgot! They are so different that it shows in their appearance to me. I don't think they look anything alike."

I looked up at her. "Yeah, you got the sexier brother," I teased.

"I don't know about that," Zoe said, looking only at Jake.

I was damn near speechless. I turned to look at Jake to see his shit-eating grin. He was just as amazed with Zoe as she was with him.

"Brook, why don't we go mix up a pitcher of margaritas?"

"Oh, that sounds good. Be right back, guys."

We both walked into the kitchen. "Have you been out there with them all night?" I asked as I snagged the ice from the freezer.

"Yes, and it's so fucking intense. I totally feel like the third wheel, but I can't help it. Aren't they adorable?" she gushed.

I chuckled. "You're not setting up two teenagers. These are grown adults. You need to give them some space. Let them talk."

She took down the tequila from the cabinet. "Oh, they haven't been holding back on my account, let me tell ya..."

"No! Please don't tell me anything that I can't un-hear."

I mixed up the drinks and Brooklyn placed the glasses and the pitcher on a tray for me to carry outside.

We each grabbed a glass and started drinking. Brooklyn's eyes wouldn't leave Jake and Zoe. It looked like she was watching a tennis match. They bounced back and forth depending on who was talking. I sat back, eating the fondue, completely uninterested in what they were even talking about. Brooklyn was far more entertaining to watch.

Many hours later, we'd made two more pitchers of margaritas. Brooklyn and I were up slowly dancing in front of the outdoor fireplace, and Jake and Zoe were sitting awfully close over in a darkened corner.

Brooklyn and I were hardly even moving. We were just holding on to one another, stealing kisses where we could.

I woke with my head pounding. I strained my eyes opened to bright light pouring into the room. I squinted against it and covered my eyes while reaching across the bed for Brook, but the bed was empty. I rolled over and fully opened my eyes. The bathroom door was ajar, giving me the perfect view of her lying on the floor, in front of the toilet, out cold.

"What the fuck is this?" someone yelled.

Who the fuck was that? It kind of sounded like Jake, but why was he here so early?

I sat up and flew out of bed toward the loud voice downstairs. I took the stairs two at a time and came to a complete stop when I saw Jake's back. He was wearing his Minion boxers again, but based on the straps going around his back, he was also wearing a bra.

I busted out laughing, doubling over because of my pounding head.

Jake spun around, discovering I was in the room. "What the fuck happened? Why am I wearing this? Help me get it off! It's cutting me in half!" He walked up to me and turned around so I could unfasten the bra.

I raised my hands, but they fell back down when another round of laughter racked my body.

"John, get this off of me before I fucking kill you," he said in a serious tone.

"Okay, okay."

I raised my hands again and wedged my fingers between his back and the tight strap. "I can't believe I'm taking a bra off my own brother. I didn't know you liked to play dress up, Jake."

"Fuck off, John."

I unsnapped the bra, and he tore his way out of the thing. It left a thick red mark around his middle.

I leaned against the wall, wiping my hand down my face because I haven't been this hungover in years.

"What the hell happened last night? I don't remember anything," Jake said, pulling me away from my thoughts.

I opened my eyes and burst out laughing again.

"Ha, ha, ha," he mocked.

I shook my head, pointing at his face while falling over to sit down on the bottom step.

"What are you laughing about now? This?" He held up the bra; it dangled off his finger at his side.

I kept shaking my head, holding my side that hurt from all the laughing. "Have you seen your face?"

"What? What's wrong with my face?" He took a few steps over to a mirror that was hanging on the wall.

"Are you fucking kidding me?" he yelled.

More laughter fell from my lips.

"Who did this to me?" He stepped back in front of me, and I got a clear view of his hooker-blue eyeshadow and red lips. He had some kind of fancy, winged eyeliner on, and bright pink blush.

"Man, that blush does not match your skin tone at all," I said around laughs.

His brows drew together, and his jaw flexed with anger.

"What's all the noise down here?" Brooklyn asked, walking down the stairs. She saw Jake and was consumed by her own laughter.

"What happened to you, Jake?"

He pointed at his face angrily. "You mean, you didn't do this?"

She was laughing so hard she couldn't talk, so she shook her head.

"Whose bra is that?" I asked.

Zoe walked into the room, and with my question, her cheeks flushed red, and she crossed her arms over her chest. We all looked at her to see she was wearing Jake's T-shirt over her bare legs.

Brooklyn and I both gasped before we were laughing again.

"Zoe, did you do this to Jake?" Brooklyn asked.

Zoe walked deeper into the room while pushing her blonde hair away from her face. "I don't remember anything." She stopped at Jake's side. "Did we..." She looked him up and down.

A knowing look crossed his face. "What? No, we couldn't have..."

"Wait, wait, wait a minute here. Are you telling me that last night was the first time you've been laid in how long, and neither of you remember?" I asked, putting my arm around his neck. "Man, that's never good."

He brushed my arm off. "No. No, we didn't. Right?" He squinted his eyes at Zoe.

"Mommy!" L.J. ran into the room, followed by Matthew who was carrying Jack.

"Daddy!" she screeched, reaching for me from Matthew's arms.

I took her and turned back to the weird situation I always find myself in. Zoe had hightailed it out of the room, and Jake was standing there holding the bra behind his back with his head down so Matthew didn't see his face.

"How were they, Dad?" Brooklyn asked, hugging L.J.

"Great, as always. We played a few games, ate a midnight snack, and slept on the couch. What the hell happened here last night?" he asked, looking at Jake.

Jake finally met his eyes. "That's what we were just trying to figure out, sir."

Matthew laughed as he got a full view of Jake's face. "I don't know if I should call you Jake or Jackie. You make one ugly woman. Do you know that?"

He tightened his lips into a straight line while nodding once.

Matthew looked at Brooklyn and pointed at Jake. "Did you do this?"

She shook her head. "I really didn't! Why does everyone ask me that?"

He turned and looked at Jake. "Did you do this to yourself?" he whispered.

"What? No!"

Matthew held his hands up, palms facing outward. "I need to get back to my office. I'm expecting a call, and honestly, I feel a little weird standing next to you."

I'm pulled from my thoughts when my tires hit the rumble strip on the side of the road. I laugh as I shake my head to clear it. That was one hell of a first impression. Zoe was so embarrassed that she almost didn't come back to work. Brooklyn had to promise that we would never speak of it again. That and shit like that happens to us all of the time for some reason. She even made her feel a little better by telling her about the time that I ate beef-flavored pain pills and preceded to make an ass out of myself at a buffet. I haven't gone to a buffet-style restaurant since.

I finally pull back up at the house and head straight to my office and sit down at the computer. I hack my way into the traffic cameras and notice, to my surprise, there is nothing. I expected to at least see the vehicle that pulled into the lot. Maybe some masked men or something. But the cameras only pick up the very corner of the lot, focusing more on the street than the surrounding areas.

"Fuck," I mumble as I push away from the computer. I lean my head back against the chair. How in the hell am I going to get into this prison, get Knox, and get out with him without being caught?

A thought quickly crosses my mind. It's damn near impossible, but it's worth a shot. I pick up the phone and call Matthew.

"Hello?" he answers on the first ring.

"Good afternoon, sir. How are you doing?"

"Great. I'm in the middle of a golf tournament though, John. Is there something you need?"

"There is, I'm afraid. Shit has hit the fan again."

I hear everything around him go quiet. "What do you mean? Are Brooklyn and the kids okay?"

"Yes, they're fine. It's my brother. He's been abducted. It's Knox, sir."

"Knox? Are you sure?"

"Absolutely. He called us from a minimum-security prison. He's been moved, and he wants out. He's holding Jake for ransom. I have to break him out of prison, and Brooklyn has to find the cure to Alzheimer's, or he's going to kill him."

"Shit! How do you get yourself into these messes?"

I let out a long breath. "I'm never going to escape my past completely, sir. I think we all knew it could come back to bite us in the ass."

"What do you need from me?" he asks, trying his hardest to help.

"I've been doing a little research on the prison. There's no way in. The only way I'm going to be able to pull this off is if I'm allowed inside. I need a job. I thought you could pull some strings."

"Are you telling me you're actually thinking about going through with this hair-brained idea?"

I shrug like he can actually see me. "It's that or let my brother die. I've been out of the game so long now that I don't know any of the current players. I have no idea who took Jake or how to find them. I hacked my way through the traffic cams, hoping to come up with something, but the trail ran cold. You know what Knox is capable of. Who's to say he will stop at Jake? What if he gets impatient and the next person he takes is Brooklyn or one of the kids? I can't let that happen."

I hear his long breath. "All right, all right. I know you're right. I'll see what I can do. Send me all the info on the prison, and I'll dig around and see if there is anyone in the area that owes me a favor."

"Thank you, sir."

"John, don't let anything happen to my daughter or grandkids. Promise me."

"I promise. I'd die before I let someone touch them."

CHAPTER EIGHT
Brooklyn

"Is that my dad on the phone?" I say, barreling into John's office. He nods and hands me the phone.

"Dad, how would you like to take the kids to Disneyland for a week?" He's been dying to take them. "I'll make all the arrangements, and the nanny will go with you."

"I would love that," he replies.

"Okay, I'll get back with you once I have it all set up. Love you, Dad."

"Love you too, Brooky."

I hang up and walk around the desk, sitting on John's lap.

"What was that all about?" He plants a kiss on my lips.

"I think Zoe and I are onto something. I don't want the kids here in case all hell breaks loose again." I kiss him this time. "What were you talking about with my dad?"

"He's going to pull some strings and get me a job in Knox's prison."

"I like the sound of that a hell of a lot better than you breaking inside."

His fingers unbutton my blouse. "The only thing I want to break inside of right now is you." His lips land on the soft skin of my neck. "I need something to feel normal right now to distract me from the shit storm that is about to happen."

"I have a million other things I need to be doing right now," I say, but push myself closer to him.

"We can make it quick." His lips have moved to the swell of my breasts, and his cock is hard underneath me.

"Pull your jeans below your hips," I say as I stand and remove my pants.

He lowers his pants and sits back down, reaching for the string on my purple lace panties. "Mmm...these are my favorite flavor." He takes both his hands and places them on either side of my hips, and his teeth find the small string on the side of my panties.

"Brook, I ordered everything...Oh my God, I'm so sorry." Zoe covers her eyes. John scrambles to pull his pants back up, and I can do nothing but laugh.

"It's not funny," he whispers through gritted teeth.

"Oh, please, like Jake hasn't caught us several times and I've seen him with morning wood tented under his Minion boxers." I casually lean down and put my pants back on.

"That's not the same," he says.

"Oh, really? And why is that?" I cross my arms over my chest.

"Because...she's...well." He's flustered. "My pants were down," he finally says.

"I didn't see a thing," Zoe says with her hand still covering her eyes. "Except, maybe, Brooklyn is a lucky girl." She laughs.

I laugh with her, but John is beet red. "Why are you still standing there?" he yells.

"I need Brooklyn to double-check to see if there is anything I missed. It's all being delivered overnight." She holds out a piece of paper in front of her.

"You can uncover your eyes now," I tell her. John adjusts himself in his jeans and huffs past her. Zoe winks at him as he walks by. I burst out laughing again and take the paper from her.

"I really am sorry about walking in on the two of you."

"It's okay. We should be focused on Jake and not John's...well, you know what I mean." I sit in the chair that John vacated. "You work fast," I say, flipping through the papers.

She sits on the leather chair across from the desk. "I think you're really onto something. I just wish we didn't have to rush and that Jake's life wasn't at stake. I hate for our hard work to be handed over to a man like Knox."

"We'll get Jake back, and then we'll deal with the rest. At least a cure will be out there for everyone. Knox has no control over that part, and we'll have Jake back."

"I hope you're right."

"Look, I'm making arrangements for the kids to go to Disneyland with my dad and the nanny for a week. Any chance I can talk you into going with them to stay out of harm's way?"

"No way in hell. With the two of us working on this together, we will figure it out sooner, and the sooner we do, Jake will be back."

"All right. Let me make some phone calls and purchase some airline tickets, then I'll get the nanny to pack the kids' bags."

"I'm going to go back to the lab and do some more research on ultrasound waves. I'll make a pot of coffee because it's going to be a long night." She stands.

"I'll meet you there when I'm done. Keep a phone on you at all times and lock the door to the lab behind you." She nods and leaves the office.

I spend the next hour making all the arrangements for them to leave tomorrow morning. I call my dad back and give him all the specifics. He still has personal bodyguards that travel with him, so I feel the kids will be safe.

After I get off the phone with him, I go searching for John. I find him in the living room, with his laptop on the coffee table. There is a picture of Jake covering his screen.

"You okay?" I ask, sitting next to him.

"Yeah. I was just thinking about everything he and I have been through together. He's always been there for me, but my life has caused him nothing but trouble."

I run my hand through his mop of hair. "Jake loves you. I think he secretly enjoys the danger as much as you do."

"I don't enjoy it anymore — not since you and the kids. What if he never gets to see his daughter because of me?"

"This isn't your fault." I wrap my arms around his neck and curl into his lap. "You gave up that life and have created a different life for all of us."

"Yeah, but it keeps biting me in the ass."

"I want to be the only thing biting your ass," I tease and wiggle my hips.

"Where's Zoe?" He looks around the room.

"She left to go to the lab." I run my hand down his hard chest.

Lightning fast, he has me flat on the couch with his body covering mine. Our hands are moving quickly to undress each other. You'd think by the way we act, we never get to have sex. He pushes my blouse over my shoulders as my hand sinks inside his pants. His raw hunger for me is overwhelming, and it sets off an alarm in my head. Is he afraid of losing me? Or, should I be afraid of losing him? His mouth between my legs halts all thoughts other than the orgasm that is already looming over me.

His phone vibrates across the coffee table. "Fuck!" he yells and leans up.

"No, don't answer it. Go back to what you were doing," I pant.

He snatches it off the table and shows me my dad's face on the screen. "That's one way to kill the mood." I jerk my blouse back over my shoulder.

"I have to take it. He's calling me back about the job at the prison."

I sit and listen as he talks to my dad and makes notes on his laptop. The scowl between his brows gets deeper and deeper, and that vein in his neck popping out. Tension is rolling off him. He hangs up the phone and lowers his head down with his hands on either side of his face.

"Hey, you can do this, and Jake's going to be okay." I rub his shoulder.

"I don't want to be his pawn anymore. What if Jake is just the tip of the iceberg and he really has something else planned for me?"

"You're afraid of losing us again, aren't you?"

He looks up, and I see tears filling his eyes. "I will do whatever I have to do to save Jake, but if I have to kill Knox in the meantime, then that's what I'll do. I can't let him control my life again. I won't go back to doing his dirty work."

"I won't let him take you again. We'll all fight him this time. Is that what all that was about a few minutes ago? I felt like you were going to climb inside me and at the same time, it felt like goodbye. I refuse to do goodbye with you again."

"When I wake up in the mornings...that split second before my eyes open, I think I've lost you." I can see the rawness in his admission tightening around his jaw. "With all of this happening again..." He gulps down his tears.

"You feel like you are going to lose us," I finish his words, and he nods. It breaks my heart to see him cry. He is the strongest man I know, and he's afraid. It makes me realize just how much he truly loves his family. He would risk anything to save us, including his entire life again.

CHAPTER NINE

John

While the kids are occupied by the nanny and Brooklyn works toward the cure, I take the time to fire up the grill. This will be the last family dinner we have before all this really starts. Matthew should be on his way home soon, and he, the kids, and the nanny will be leaving first thing in the morning. I also need to figure out a backup plan in case Matthew's recommendation doesn't go through to land me the job. The weight of the unknown is heavy, and the fact that my brother's life is on the line is only putting me on edge.

But for now, I refuse to acknowledge it. I have one last night with my family, and I'm going to enjoy it. I have to force myself, knowing that Jake is out there somewhere.

I dice and season the steak before pouring it over the potatoes inside the foil pouch. I pour on some seasoned garlic butter and seal the packs. While the grill heats up, I move on to making a salad.

Internally, I laugh at myself. Here I am, tossing a fucking salad with the plans of breaking someone out of prison. I really wish I could go back in time and kick my own ass for ever getting into this shit. But then it hits me—I wouldn't have Brook or my kids without living the life I had. Even if this shit does get me killed, they're all worth it, and I'd live out my whole life in captivity to keep them safe.

As I'm walking the food out to the grill, I run into Brook on her way to the house.

"Are you cooking dinner?" she asks, pausing next to me.

I nod. "Yeah. I figured this could be our last family dinner for a while. I wanted it to be special."

Her head cocks to the side, and a look of sadness washes over her before she reaches for me. Her hands tangle into my shirt, and I allow her to pull me closer. Her blue eyes meet mine. "I don't want to hear you talk this way. Everything will be fine. We've been through this before."

I can't help the laugh that escapes me.

Her brows pull together. "Why are you laughing?"

I shake my head. "Shouldn't I be the one reassuring you?" I place my hand on the side of her face, cupping her cheek as I look longingly into her eyes. "You're so strong and fearless. I don't know what I'd do without you."

She smiles before placing her hand on mine. "Good thing you won't ever have to." She presses her lips against mine quickly. "Now, get my dinner done so I can get back to work." She pulls away with a giggle, and I swat her on the ass for her smart-ass remark.

I toss everything on the grill and go inside to set the table. Normally, our dinner isn't anything big. Half the time, I eat standing up while pouring milk and picking up forks that have been dropped, but tonight I set the big table in the dining room. I use the best plates, glasses, and silverware. I even light a few candles to place in the center.

In the corner of the room is a drink cart, and I make sure everything we will need to drink is there so that nobody has to leave the room. I want at least an hour of uninterrupted time with my family.

Even though Matthew is no longer in the presidency, Brooklyn works undercover, and I am no longer on the *call to place your hit* list, we're usually still pretty busy. All of our phones are always ringing, and it's something that Brooklyn hates. I take out a basket that's used every Thanksgiving and Christmas to place your phone into before entering the dining room and set it down on the table outside the dining room door. Anytime this basket is setting outside this door, everyone knows what to do, and they don't even bother arguing it anymore. They know Brooklyn won't serve anyone anything until all the phones are accounted for.

Matthew walks in the front door, dropping his bags on the floor. "Where are my grandkids?" he asks when they don't come barreling toward him.

I look up from the wine I'm pouring. "They are with the nanny, but they should be coming in at any minute. Are you excited about your Disneyland trip?"

He lets out a jolly laugh. "You know I am. I've been trying to talk Brooklyn into letting me take them for months now."

"Want a glass of wine before dinner?"

One of his brows raises as he looks me over. "Let's save the wine for dinner. What do you say to taking me into the office and pouring me a stiff drink? It's going to be a long flight."

I look at the time on my watch, checking to make sure I have a few minutes until I need to take the food off the grill. "All right and then you can brief me on my new job."

"I didn't say you had the job. I'm good, but not that good. I got you an interview. It's up to you to get the job."

I lead him into the office and walk over to the drink cart in the corner, pouring us both a glass of bourbon.

"They haven't called yet," I say, handing over his glass and taking a seat behind my desk with my own. "I don't know what I'll do if I don't get the job. I mean, would you want to break into a prison, find one person in a sea of hundreds, then break back out? I don't want to be the first dumbass to go to prison for breaking into a prison."

He laughs as he takes a sip. "I don't blame you there. I'm sure it will all work out, John. I know how stressed you can get about things like this, but you need to believe in yourself."

I'm so tired of hearing everyone say this. "I was a hitman. I wasn't some expert at breaking and entering. Give me a gun, I can hit the target every time, but break into a highly guarded prison that's covered in security cameras, guards, and a twelve-foot electric fence?"

"What's your plan if you get the job? How do you plan on getting him out of there? Never mind, don't tell me. I don't need to be involved in the plotting of a crime."

I chuckle. "Well, that's good because I have no fucking clue. This is fucking useless. Maybe I should be focusing on trying to find whoever took Jake and working on getting him back instead of feeding into this web of bullshit."

"There is something. I mean, I'm sure I can get a detailed list of Knox's visitors. Maybe even security footage of his visitors and lawyer meetings. It would be something we could do while we wait to see about the job at the prison."

I nod. "Okay. It's worth a shot anyway," I reply.

"I'll make some calls." He places his empty glass on the edge of the desk before standing and walking out of the room.

I lean back in my chair, thinking everything over. Breaking Knox out of prison won't just be a problem. It will be a lifetime of running and hoping the authorities don't track me down. And Matthew can't bail me out this time. If I get caught, I'm done for. I'll be spending the rest of my life in prison. All I can do is pray that we can get around Knox and find my brother. Then Brooklyn wouldn't be under any pressure to find this cure. I also need to gather evidence that Knox is attempting to break out, putting him back in max and limiting his contact so he can't put a hit out on us. I refuse to wreck my family's lives by packing them up and keeping them in hiding from the rest of the world. If these kids deserve anything, it's a shot at a normal life.

I'm pulling the food off the grill when I hear the kids' feet stomping their way through the house. They run out the back door. Jack automatically goes straight to the swing set, but L.J. runs up to me. "We had so much fun today! We went to the park and then had ice cream. Then we went to Splash World!"

I laugh at his excitement. "That's awesome, buddy! I think Mommy has some more fun things planned for you. Why don't you go get her out of her office so we can eat dinner."

"Okay!" he yells before running off.

I turn off the grill and grab the tray. "Come on, Jack. Let's get cleaned up for dinner."

She jumps off her swing, being the little daredevil she is, and runs up to my side.

"Will you open the door for me, princess?"

"Sure, Daddy." The sweetness of her voice could stop my heart.

Everyone comes in, and the kids get washed up. We all drop our phones in the basket as we head into the dining room.

"This is so nice of you, John," Zoe says, taking her seat at the table.

"You did a beautiful job at setting the table, babe." Brooklyn presses a kiss to my cheek. "Now that I know what you're capable of, you can do this every Thanksgiving and Christmas." She laughs as she helps Jack up into the chair.

I mock a laugh back at her as I place the food on the table. I feel guilty knowing Jake is not here.

Brooklyn and I help the kids make their plates then we pass around the dinner rolls and salad.

"I should have everything we need after dinner, John," Matthew says as he takes the bowl of salad Brooklyn is passing him.

"What do you need?" she asks, looking at me.

"Your dad suggested while we wait to hear back from the prison that we look into Knox's visitors and phone calls. Maybe try to figure out who took Jake."

"That's a good idea, Dad. If we can get to Jake without having to deal with Knox, there wouldn't be any real pressure to get this cure done right away. I mean, I think we're close, but it's going to need proper testing and years of study to make sure the disease doesn't come back."

I place my hand over hers that's setting on top of the table. "It could mean a lot of things. Let's just keep our fingers crossed. But in the meantime, do you want to tell the kids where they're going tomorrow?"

Brook smiles as she looks over at the kids who are picking at their salad. "You guys are going to go with Grandpa and Grace to Disneyland!"

They scream and clap their hands and bounce up and down in their seats, showing their excitement.

I look at their smiling faces, and my heart swells with love for these two kids. They are perfect, and I couldn't have asked for a better life. I've gotten so much more than I deserved when it comes to my family. I never thought I'd be this lucky. I only pray that Jake can hold on a little bit longer. I want him to have this feeling about his family. I want him to know the power of love when it comes to your child. I know he loves L.J. and Jack as his own, but nothing beats the feeling of holding that little baby in your arms for the first time. I won't allow him to miss out on that.

CHAPTER TEN
Jake

I've been held captive three days now. I scratch lines into the concrete with the cross of my necklace that hangs from a black leather braided band. A few rays of sun glimmer through the small window. As I lay my head back against the wall, I run my hand over the scruff on my face. My beard has gotten thick fairly quickly. I remember a time I didn't have to shave because of the chemo treatments.

This is all so fucked up. I want to be angry at John for always getting me caught up in his shit, but I can't be. If it wasn't for him and Brooklyn, I would have died years ago from the cancer that was eating up my body. I would have never met Zoe and had a baby on the way, but when will this shit ever end? Or will it? If John has figured out by now that it is Knox that's controlling the cards, he will kill him. John has worked so hard to have a normal life.

I know at one time, killing came easy for him, but now, I think it might destroy him. He's a good husband and father. He doesn't want his children tainted by his past, and neither do I.

Pushing off the wall, I look around again for any way to escape. The window is too narrow for me to fit through and so are the bars. Since they captured me for the second time, they've come down here in pairs. One of them is always sporting a gun at me.

Leaning on the wall, I run both my hands through my hair and squeeze my eyes tight, trying to think. I know Knox is behind this, but what does he want from Brooklyn? Has she discovered another cure? How would he know? And why wouldn't he go after her like before? He must be using me for leverage to get what he wants from her and John.

Maybe he's sick and thinks Brooklyn can cure him of what ails him. Brooklyn will do whatever he wants to save me. I know her. Me trying to find out what he wants won't do any good. The only thing that will help Brooklyn is me getting free of them. I just have to figure out how to not die in the process.

Gravel crunches underneath tires outside next to the window. I stand on my tiptoes and pull myself up with my fingers using the ledge. Two men wearing all-black clothing get out. One of them is carrying what looks like some sort of hunting rifle. I can only make out muffled voices when the two men that have been guarding me exchange words with them before they get into the SUV.

I let myself slide down the wall. I guess it was a changing of the guards. Maybe these two don't know they have to come down here two at a time. Glancing at my watch, it's almost lunchtime. They've been bringing me two meals a day. One around eleven in the morning, the other at seven at night. The meals both consist of stale bread with lunch meat. If I ever get out of here, I don't think I will ever eat a sandwich again. They bring me two bottles of water with each meal. They must not want me to die of thirst. They might not get their money for kidnapping me if I die.

That's it! I'll pretend to be sick. They need me alive so they would have to get me some help.

When I hear footsteps near the stairs, I lie facedown on the floor. The hinges on the door creak as it opens. Both men descend down the wooden stairs. I close my eyes as they get closer and moan.

"Ohhh." I curl into a ball on my side. I repeat the moaning several times.

One of them unlocks the door, and the other walks by him and lays down a tray of food. He has the rifle draped over his shoulder. He nudges me with his boot.

"Eat your food," he says.

"My gut feels like it's on fire," I moan again.

"You're faking. Now sit up and eat," he barks.

I roll over, facing the other way. Arching up, I stick my finger down my throat and start gagging.

"I don't think he's faking, man," the other guard says. "We need to call someone."

They both step just outside my cell. I roll back over to be able to see them. The bigger of the two men, the one with the rifle, pulls a cell phone out of his shirt pocket.

"He's sick. What do you want us to do with him?" He pauses and listens. "I don't know what the fuck is wrong with him. He says his gut feels like it's on fire and then he started puking."

I moan loudly. "Aw! It feels like an alien is coming out!" Dramatic I know, but I want to freak them out.

"Can you hear him?" He holds the phone out in my direction, and I moan again.

He places it back next to his ear. "He needs a doctor." He listens again.

"I didn't sign up to take care of someone. Do you want me to kill him and put him out of his misery? That I will willingly do."

Maybe I shouldn't be such a good actor. I curl back into a ball but stay quiet this time.

"Okay, I know the address," he finally says and puts his phone back in his pocket.

"What did he say?" the other guard asks him.

"There is a small-town doctor on the next island over. We are going to take him there." He unlocks the gate, then hauls me up off the floor by the arm.

I hold my stomach as we go up the stairs. The cut on my foot is still tender while walking in my socked feet. It really hurts when it lands on the gravel outside as they shove me into the back seat of the SUV. One man slides in beside me as the other gets behind the wheel.

"What are we going to tell the doctor about him?" The man in the back seat looks nervous.

"We aren't going to tell him anything. I'll hold a gun to his head, and he will do as I ask."

Gravel flies out as he takes off down the drive. He pushes a remote button to open the gate. Leaning my head against the window, I keep one eye open to make note of where we are. About a mile down the road is a long, narrow bridge that leads to another island. One that I recognize. We are still in the Hawaiian Islands. The one we are driving to is two islands over from where I live. There is only one doctor on this island, and I took L.J. to him one time when Brooklyn was sick. I hope to God that he recognizes me. He's an older gentleman with a small, busy family practice. Most of the neighboring islanders come here to see him.

The familiar blue building comes into view as we clear the bridge. There are several cars in the dirt parking lot when we park. The man in the front gets out and lays his rifle in the seat. "Stay here," he barks and walks away. I see him place his hand on the handle of his gun that is sticking out of the back of his black jeans.

A few minutes later, he returns to the SUV and opens the back door. "Get out!" He pulls his gun out and waves it at me. "The kind lady at the front desk has agreed to bring him in the back door."

"How did you manage that?" the other guy asks as he opens my door and helps me out.

"I told her that the patient was too sick to wait in the waiting room and he would throw up all over the floor." He laughs.

A woman greets us at the back door and puts the three of us in a small room. She tries to get them to wait outside as she helps me sit on the table.

"I have some phone calls to make," the big guy says and then whispers something to the other man, who sits down in a metal folding chair.

The cute brunette medical assistant hands me a gown. "My name is Sara, Mister..."

"Smith," the guy in the chair says.

The young girl smiles sweetly at me. "Put this on, Mr. Smith. The doctor will be in shortly to see you." She turns and closes the door behind her.

"You let me do the talking!" the guard growls. "If you say one thing that gives you away, I will kill that pregnant wife of yours."

I remain quiet as I remove my shirt and put the gown on. I leave my jeans on but take my dirty, bloody sock off my foot. If I'm going to escape, I'm going to need it taken care of while I'm here.

"What are you doing?" He points to my foot. "We're here for your stomachache."

"Well, my foot hurts too. You wouldn't want it getting infected and me to die from it, would you?"

That seems to appease him. He pats the gun under his jacket. "Don't make me kill the only doc in town."

As I sit back on the table, there is a knock on the door, and the doctor walks in. "Hi, Mr. Smith," he says, glancing down at the chart. "I'm Dr. Tinsley." His eyebrows draw together as he shakes my hand. "Have you been in here before?"

"No, he's a tourist. Never been here before," the man in the chair says.

Dr. Tinsley looks at him and then at me. "I don't see anything written in this chart other than you have a severe stomachache." He flips it open.

"Yeah, I think it's something that I ate." I glare at the guard. "Actually, the pain has let up some since earlier."

"Lay back and let me examine you," the doctor says. I lie back as he washes his hands, dries them, and then dons a pair of gloves. He pulls up my paper gown and presses on my stomach. "Does this hurt?"

"A little."

"Show me where it was hurting earlier."

I want to make up something so that he will have to call an ambulance, but I'm afraid if I do, my friend here will start shooting up the place and kill innocent people. "Right here." I put my hand just below my belly button.

He presses. "Is it still tender?"

"Only a little." I sit. "But this hurts like a son of a bitch." I draw my foot up and show him my heel.

"This redness here indicates that it's infected." He points to the area around the cut. "What did you cut it on?"

"He stepped on some glass," the guard answers.

"How long ago?" The guard starts to answer him, but the doctor puts his hand up to stop him. "Mr. Smith is more than capable of answering my questions.

I want to smirk at him. "Three days ago," I say, instead.

His eyes search mine for a minute. I really think he's trying to place me, but the scruff on my face isn't helping. I rub my hand over my beard, hoping to give him a hint that it's not always there.

"Well, it's too late for me to stitch it up, but I can clean it then dress it. You will need to take some antibiotics for a week and then come see me again." He opens a drawer and pulls out some gauze. Then he sticks his head out and calls for Sara to come help him.

I lie back on the table, and she places a white towel under my feet.

"Sir, we are going to need a little room. Would you please go sit in the waiting room?" the doctor asks the guard.

He hesitates but gets up. He points a finger at me. "I'll be outside the door."

The doctor waits until the door is closed before he starts working on my foot. His assistant hands him whatever he needs. As he is cleaning it, he asks me a question.

"Is there anything else you need, Mr. Smith, while you are here?"

I look past him at the door and then back at him. I make a motion with my hand for pen and paper. Sara nods and pulls both out of her pocket.

I scribble down John's number and write, "Stand by Me. Two islands over, come and find me."

The doorknob rattles, and I stuff the pen and paper in Sara's pocket. She steps back toward the sink.

"Are you almost done in here?" The guard sticks his head inside the room.

"Just finishing up," the doctor says as he rolls the gauze around my foot. "You need to keep this clean. Sara can get you the antibiotics to take with you from the front desk." He turns to her. "Why don't you take this gentleman to get them while I finish up in here."

The guard scowls but follows Sara.

"Go out the back door while he's up front," the doctor whispers.

I rip the gown off and throw my shirt over my head.

"Here, take these," the doctor says as he's removing his socks and shoes.

I slip the socks on and then the shoes that are a little too big, but they will protect my feet. Then he opens the door wide and stands in the hall. He waves me out when the coast is clear. I see the other guard leaning against the SUV, talking on the phone. I take off in a sprint heading down the road.

He sees me, and I hear the car door open. I pick up my pace, and as I turn into one of the alleys, something pierces me in the ass. I don't slow down to look as I try to climb the fence between the buildings. I reach up with my arms, but my legs don't follow. I look behind me, and there is a dart sticking out of my left butt cheek. I yank it out and try to climb again, but instead, I hit the pavement beneath me.

CHAPTER ELEVEN

John

Matthew was right. By the time dinner is over and we have everything cleaned up and the kids in bed, the files have been sent over. Brooklyn goes back to work in her home office, while Matthew and I stay holed up in mine. We have files upon files of audio, video, and visitor logs.

I know Knox isn't stupid. There is no way he openly talked about his plan over a phone call he knew was being listened to. If he disclosed his plan to anyone, it would have been done in person or over his private cell phone that he managed to sneak in.

We start watching the hours of video from visiting hours. It looks like the camera is in the far corner of the room, getting a view from every inmate. We can clearly see Knox and the person he's talking to, but there is no audio. While Matthew watches the video, claiming he can read lips, I get to work on doing a search on every name on the visitor log.

Many of the names seem to be from friends and family, and nothing comes up when looking through them.

"I got it!" Matthew says.

"You got what?" I ask, not bothering to look away from my computer screen as I start another search.

"Right here, he says, 'it's done. We have a captain.'"

I look up. "That doesn't even make sense. Why would they need a captain?"

He looks closer at the screen. "Maybe he says, 'we have him captured.'"

I push away from my desk and lean over Matthew, wanting a look for myself. "Well, what's he saying now?"

Matthew gets quiet as he looks closer. "Our plane is in motion."

"You mean, our plan is in action?" I ask.

"Yeah, maybe that's it." Matthew smiles to himself.

"What's the date and time on this visit?" I ask, moving back to my chair.

"Time is 2:05 p.m. on June twelfth."

I look at the logs and find the name of the visitor: Haku Kaiwi. I spin around and type the name into my computer, pulling up a long list of crimes he's been convicted of, property records, and much more.

"I think I found something," I say as I continue clicking my way around.

Matthew stands up and leans over to view the screen.

"Are you seeing what I'm seeing?"

"It looks like Kaiwi owns land a few islands over."

"That could be where they're keeping Jake." I pull up a satellite of the property but don't see anything out of the ordinary. My best guess—if Jake is there, they are keeping him underground, in a basement or cellar of some sort.

It's a long shot, but it's better than nothing. I push away from my desk, heading toward the door.

"What are you doing? You're just going to drive over there and do this by yourself? What if you get taken too?"

"If I can get Jake myself, Knox won't have any leverage on me. He can spend the rest of his days rotting in his cell. I'm better alone."

Matthew shakes his head while rubbing his brows. "Let me send some men in with you."

"No. I don't want anyone in my way. I don't want to be out there distracted, wondering if I'm going to have to tell a woman that the man she loves isn't coming home. I work better alone, you know that." I turn to leave, but he grabs hold of my bicep.

"And I don't want to have to tell my daughter and grandkids that you're not coming home because I let you walk out that door alone."

We're in some sort of standoff. I understand where he's coming from, but my mind is always sharper when I'm alone, when there is nobody else there to worry about other than myself.

"Matthew, I know what you're saying, but I'm more comfortable alone. I won't put anyone else in danger, and that's final." I leave the room quickly before he can stop me.

I head straight for Brooklyn. I know if I don't, he will only do it himself and make her agree with him. I open the door and find Zoe curled up on the sofa.

"I think I know where they are keeping him," I say, walking past Zoe to Brooklyn.

"Where?" Her gaze pops up to mine.

"A few islands over. I'm going there now." I turn to leave, in a hurry to save my brother, but Brooklyn calls after me.

"John!"

I turn around to face her. I should have known it wouldn't be this easy.

"You're going now? You know nothing about these people or this place. What if they have traps or alarms set up? You need to dig a little instead of closing your eyes and jumping."

"They have Jake," I tell her. That's all the digging I need to do.

"She's right, John. I want to save Jake as much as you do but getting yourself killed won't do that. You need to learn the layout, find all the exit points, learn who we're dealing with and what their weaknesses are. We need to come up with a plan instead of going in blind," Zoe says.

Matthew busts through the door, panting. When he sees I'm already here, he flops down on the couch. "I guess he told you what he plans on doing?" he asks Brook.

She nods. "He did. Zoe and I are trying to talk him out of it."

"Good. He needs help. He can't do this all alone. It's too dangerous. But you know his stubborn ass. He won't listen to me."

Brooklyn glares at me. "You're planning on going in alone?"

I look over at her. "Can we go somewhere private and talk, please?"

She takes a deep breath but walks outside. I follow after her.

The second I'm outside with the door closed, she's jumping on me. "Are you seriously thinking of doing this alone?"

"You know me, Brook. I work better alone. My mind is clearer when I don't have to think of anyone but myself. You want Jake back, let me do this."

She starts pacing with her arms crossed over her chest. "And what happens if you're captured too? Then what?"

I walk up to her, stopping her pacing. "That won't happen. I'll get out of there, with or without Jake. I'll be back. If the place is too guarded, I'll come home and get help. I won't put myself in danger. I promise." I place my hands on her biceps and rub up and down.

I can see her wavering. "John..."

I grab her against me, landing a firm kiss on her lips. When I pull away, I say, "I love you, Brook. I love those kids in there. No way am I not coming back."

"When are you leaving?"

"I'm going to take your advice and do a little research on who I'm messing with. Check the property over, come up with a strategy, and leave first thing in the morning. If I knew where I was going, the dark would make it easier to hide, but no way will they expect me to strike in broad daylight."

She nods. "If you get Jake, Knox is going to have a fit. You're his ticket out of there."

"I know. We'll need to be prepared for his plan B."

"I'm glad the kids will be leaving in the morning before all this goes down."

I take her hand and squeeze it. "Me too." I motion toward her office. "Come on, let's go break the news to your dad. I think he was about to have a heart attack."

She giggles. "He loves you and was just trying to protect you the only way he knows how."

"I know, and I appreciate it. I consider him as my own father." I stop her just before she opens the door. "This family—you, me, the kids, your dad, Jake, Zoe, and their baby, that's what's most important to me. I won't rest until we're all safe. I promise."

She offers up a half grin. "I know, John. We love you too."

I wake bright and early to pack up everything I'll need. I sneak into the kids' rooms and kiss them both on the head. I wish I could hang out long enough to see them off on their trip, but I need to get moving.

I kiss Brooklyn goodbye and promise to return before jumping onto my bike. It's going on eight a.m. when my phone rings. I push the button on my earpiece. "Hello?"

"Good morning, sir. This is Sara. I'm a nurse at a local practice here on the island. I have a message for you."

I slow down and pull my bike over to the side of the road. "Okay?"

"Stand by me," she says.

Jake. "I'm sorry, how did you get this message?"

"As I said, I'm a nurse. Yesterday, a man was brought in. He had two other men with him. He was hurt, and we just got this funny feeling that something else was going on. It's like, he wasn't allowed to talk for himself in fear he would give something away. The doctor asked to be alone with that patient, and he wrote down this number and that message. I'm sorry, I would have called sooner, but..."

"No, it's okay. What island did you say this was on?"

She finishes giving me the information I need, and I hang up the phone. It looks like I was right all along. The only thing is, will Jake be there? She said he got away yesterday, but did they catch him? I have to believe they did or I would have heard from him by now.

I shift into first gear and make my way back onto the road. I shift through gears like a madman, just needing to get there. It's been too long already.

CHAPTER TWELVE

Zoe

"Do you really think John will find him?" I ask as soon as Brooklyn comes back through the door.

"Yes. I just hope he doesn't get himself killed in the process."

Matthew stands. "I can still send some men after him." He embraces his daughter.

"He thinks he's better off and more focused alone, and he doesn't want to risk anyone else's life."

"The kids and I need to get going, or we're going to miss our flight. Besides, I want them out of harm's way."

"I'll run up and get them," I say.

"I really wish you would come with us," he says, releasing Brooklyn.

"I'm not going anywhere as long as Jake is missing, but I will help you get the kids going."

"Okay, Jack's things are already packed. I have a few more things I need to get for L.J."

"I've rented a van to take us to the airport. It should be here anytime," Matthew says, heading for the front door.

———

Within an hour, I'm watching Brooklyn kiss the kids as she buckles them into their car seats in the back of the van. She has tears in her eyes when she stands next to me.

"I've never been away from Jack," she says, sniffing.

"She'll be okay. She adores your father and Grace is so good with her. Besides, that little girl would follow L.J. to the moon."

"She does love her big brother."

"I hope one day when Jake and I have a couple of children, that they love each other as much as your kids do." I wrap my arm around her shoulder.

"Are you kidding me? If these kids are anything like their parents, they will be a force to be reckoned with," she says with a laugh.

"Now that the kids are out of harm's way, what's next?" I ask as we walk up the front porch steps.

"Some of the equipment we need will be here today. The rest is being delivered tomorrow."

"Why don't I go to the lab and get it all set up when it gets here?"

"I don't want you lifting anything." She points to my belly bump.

"I won't. I'll have them place it right where I want it. I need to run by the house first and pick up my research. I worked on it late last night because I couldn't sleep. I really think this is going to work."

"I'm very hopeful. I just wish I didn't have to give it to the likes of Knox."

"Regardless if Knox gets it or not, if we can pull this off, think of the lives that will be changed forever."

"You're right. I need to take Knox out of the equation. Do you want me to go to the house with you?" she asks.

"No. I'm just going to run inside to grab my research then get to the lab."

"I'll meet you there in an hour. Keep your eyes peeled for any signs of danger."

"I'll be fine. John gave me a pistol to carry with me. It's in my purse." We walk inside, and I take my bag off the counter. "I'll see you in a little while," I tell her and walk out to my car.

The short drive to my house, all I can do is think about Jake. I feel lost without him. I miss his touch and his beautiful smile. He always makes me laugh.

His arms wrapped around my belly and he splayed his hand wide. "I love this little bump," he said and kissed my neck.

"You're not the one getting fat," I said and leaned my head back on his shoulder.

"You're not fat, and I think it's sexy as hell," he said as his hands traveled to my breast.

"Mmmm, now that I like." I turned my head to the side and kissed him softly.

"I like the baby hormones too." He pressed his hard cock into my lower back.

"I think you're the one with the baby hormones. You've been insatiable ever since I told you I was pregnant." I turned in his arms, and his hands slid to my ass.

"You should stay pregnant forever." One of his hands pushed my spaghetti strap off my shoulder, and his lips landed on my collarbone.

"Unless you can get pregnant, that's not happening." I chuckled.

He stepped back. "I would look like an old man with a beer belly." He released me and walked over to the bed. He stuffed one of the decorative pillows under his shirt and walked back over to me. "See," he said, pointing at his stomach.

I couldn't help but giggle at him. "God, I hope my belly won't be that big."

He tried to wrap his arms around my waist, but the pillow got in the way. He looked between us and then bent over to look at his crotch. "How the hell is this going to work?" He pointed to his cock.

I laughed and pulled him over to the bed. "I guess we are going to have to be creative. Maybe even a little kinky." I winked at him.

"Oh, I'm liking the sound of this." He whipped the pillow from beneath his shirt. "You've got me so fucking hard talking about being kinky, we are going to start right now."

As I pull into my driveway, a piece of gravel flies up and smacks the windshield, scaring me half to death. I put the car in park and inspect the crack the rock made. I'll worry about it later. I grab my purse and keys and head inside the house. I don't know why, but as I insert the key into the painted red door, my hand shakes. A feeling of uneasiness comes over me.

As I open the door, I peek inside. Nothing looks out of place, and all I hear is quiet. I shake it off and head to my office in the back of the house. Before I take the file off my desk, I pick up the picture of Jake and me sitting on the corner. He's leaning over my shoulder with a huge smile on his face. This was taken not long after we met. I press a kiss to his face and jump when I hear a noise.

I snatch the file off the desk and put it in my purse. Taking out the pistol, I walk over to the office door and slowly close it. Just before it's closed, a large hand breaks in between the door. I scream and push as hard as I can against it.

He gets both hands in between. I lean over and bite one of his hands, and he yells out.

"You fucking bitch!"

He pushes so hard I fall back onto the floor, and the gun topples out of my hand. I quickly pick it up and get off the ground at the same time. The gun goes off, shooting him in the foot. He screams again. I'm so startled, I barely see another hooded man come into the room. He yanks the gun from me and twists my arm behind my back.

"You can't take care of a pregnant woman?" he taunts the guy on the floor.

He's twisting my arm so hard, I'm afraid it will break if I try to elbow him in the gut with my other arm. I lean forward slightly and stomp on his foot. He releases me, and I run by the man on the ground, but not before he grabs my ankle.

I'm filled with fear as I try to catch myself before the baby slams into the wooden floor. I roll to the side. My head bounces off the corner of the door, and my entire body slams down hard.

I try to get to my feet, but a wave of nausea hits me, and I'm blinded with blood dripping into my eye. I fall back over and protectively shield my belly. The man that was twisting my arm reaches down, pulls me off the floor, and shoves me through the door. The other man hobbles behind me, cursing the entire way.

"No!" I scream as he pops the trunk of his car. I fight him as hard as I can, but I'm afraid of him hurting the baby. He picks me up in his arms and roughly tosses me into the trunk. The other man holds my head down, barely getting his hand out of the way before the trunk closes.

I kick and scream, beating my fists on the inside of the trunk.

"You be quiet in there!" One of them pounds on the car. "Don't make me drug you. God knows what effects it will have on the baby!"

I still at his words. I have to protect this little one at all costs. I need to keep my wits about me. Placing the heel of my hand over my brow, I press hard trying to stop the bleeding. With my other hand, I feel around the dark trunk for anything I could use as a weapon. It's empty, not even a set of jumper cables. I feel for the edge to see if there is a compartment for a spare tire. The lip of the carpet comes up as I pry my fingers under it. Maneuvering my body so that I'm raised up as much as I can, I pull up on the carpet and reach under it, feeling for the jack. It's bolted down.

My head bumps against the trunk as the car drives over something, causing me to fall back down. I get up again and start working on loosening the bolt. It doesn't budge.

"Lefty Lucy," I tell myself and try again. I turn as hard as I can, and it finally moves. I take the bolt out and shove it into my pocket. Snaking my arm further under, I can't reach the other side. I yank at the jack, hoping it will pop off, but it won't.

I lie back down and take the bolt out of my pocket, clutching it to my body. It's not much, but maybe I can do enough damage to one of them to get free. A sharp pain in my lower belly has me gasping in pain. I curl into a fetal position and hold my belly in my hands.

"Not yet little one. It's too soon," I say, trying to breathe through the pain. Tears fill my eyes. "We are going to be okay," I chant several times, trying to convince myself.

The bumping of the car finally stops. I hear the doors open and footsteps crunching on the ground. Light floods the trunk as it opens.

"Are you going to behave, or do I need to restrain you?" a gruff voice asks.

I don't want to give them any more reason to hurt me, so I slowly climb out of the trunk. I'm surrounded by trees, and I can hear a creek flowing nearby. There is a small cabin sitting further down an overgrown pathway. Two armed men dressed in all black are standing outside the door as we approach it.

"What the hell, man? You weren't supposed to hurt her," one of them says, scowling.

"She's a feisty little bitch," the one I shot in the foot says.

The door opens, and I'm shoved inside.

"Zoe?" I hear from a voice in the dark house.

CHAPTER THIRTEEN

John

I follow the route my GPS is showing until I get to the island Jake is being held captive on. I start making my way in their direction but get off the bike when I'm still a half mile away. I stash it in the trees, pack up my rifle, ammo, and anything else I could need. There is no way I can ride my loud-ass bike right up to their front door. I want the element of surprise on my side.

I hike my rifle up on my shoulder higher as I trek through the brush, using my phone to stay on my path. I studied the surrounding land so much, I know it like the back of my hand. I know exactly where I need to hide to make sure I'm not seen. My plan is to take out the guard by the door and make my way into the house. From there, I'll take out anyone in my way.

I'm still a good quarter mile away from the property when the phone in my hand vibrates. I look down at the screen and see a picture of Matthew. What the fuck? Doesn't he know I'm in the middle of something here?

"Hello?" I answer.

"Hi, Daddy! We're getting on an airplane!" Jack cheers.

I let out a quiet laugh. "That's great, princess. Can I talk to Papa?"

"Okay. I love you, Daddy."

"I love you too. Be careful and have fun."

"Hello?" Matthew picks up the phone.

"How's everything going?"

"Great. We're just about to board. Jack wouldn't stop until she called you. I hope we didn't mess anything up for you."

"Don't worry about it. I'm standing in the middle of the fucking woods, about a quarter mile away."

"All right. Take care, John."

"I will. Take care of my kids," I tell him before hanging up.

When the call ends, the map is back on my screen.

Hearing Jack's sweet little voice brought me back to daddy mode. I was in killer mode. It's so strange how I can switch between the two so easily. I haven't done this in such a long time, I didn't realize I had it in me anymore. I have so much to lose now — her voice reminded me of that. Fear and dread settle over me.

I try to push it to the back of my mind and shift back into gear mentally. I can't be thinking about my family while I'm doing this. It will distract me, and I need to be sharp. I admit, doing this job was a lot easier when I only had myself to think about — that's why I preferred to be alone. But meeting Brooklyn, she opened up a whole new set of doors for me. She gave me something I didn't know I needed: a life, a real life with family, friends, and love.

My phone vibrating pulls me back to the here and now, and I look down to see that I'm nearing the location. I slide the phone into my pocket and slowly move on. I'm getting closer now, so I need to move slow and precise. I don't want to make too much noise to alert them.

I make my way to the edge of the property and pull the rifle off my shoulder. Using the scope, I start looking around, getting to know my surroundings. I'm not even fifteen feet from the door, so I know if there is some kind of silent alarm, they should be coming out any minute. The place is quiet — too quiet. There is a blacked-out SUV in the drive, but no guard at the door and I don't see any movement in the house.

The house is surrounded by nothing but overgrown wilderness, not a neighbor for miles. This would be the perfect place to hold him. But if Jake was inside, they would have a guard, right?

I decide to test the waters. I grab a thin tree branch and snap it off. A dog that's chained up next to the house starts barking. I raise my rifle again. I aim the gun at the door while looking through my scope as I wait.

The screen door flies open, smacking the side of the house. An older man comes out, rounds the house, and begins scolding the dog for being loud. Slowly, I start walking up behind him. I could shoot, but what if I'm in the wrong place and kill an innocent man? I'll ask him a few questions. With this rifle in my hands, there is no way he won't answer.

When I'm standing directly behind him, I clear my throat. He spins around to face me and the second his eyes lock on mine, the anger on his face is replaced by surprise.

"Who the hell are you, and why the fuck are you on my property?" the man asks, not fazed at all by the rifle I'm pointing at him.

"My name is John, and I have some questions for you." I use my weapon to motion back toward the house.

He looks from the house, to me, and back to the house before walking in that direction. He leads me into his home, and he sits at the small kitchen table. I lower my weapon, put it back on my shoulder, and take out my handgun. I sit down at the table and make sure the gun is always pointed at him.

"Where's my brother?"

"I don't know what you're talking about." He waves his hand in front of his face, dismissing the question.

"My brother, Jake Remington, has been missing for several days now. He's being used as leverage against me to do something for a very bad person. I tracked him back to this house." I raise the gun higher and cock it. The sound of the bullet going into the chamber cuts through the silence. "Now, tell me what you know."

It looks like he's biting the inside of his cheek while he thinks it over. His gray eyes bounce around the room from object to object but never land on me.

I stand quickly, causing my chair to screech off the dirty tiled floor. I'm towering over him now with only the wooden table between us. "Don't make me ask again," I say as I raise the gun and aim it directly at his head.

His Adam's apple bobs as he swallows. "He's not here. He's been moved — him and that pregnant wife of his."

"Zoe?" My heart begins pounding in my chest. How the fuck was she taken? When? Does Brooklyn know? Is she all right?

"Where are they?" I ask with my eyes squinting together. I'm trying my hardest to control my anger, to keep myself in check so I don't shoot this man. I know he's not innocent, but I don't need more blood on my hands. They've been painted red long enough.

He reaches across the table and takes a piece of paper and a pencil. He quickly scribbles the address down and slides it over.

I pick it up and study it, realizing that it's not too much further. I stuff the paper into my pocket. "I'm going to let you live, but if they aren't where you say they are, I'm coming back to put this gun in your mouth. You hear me?"

He nods. "Don't worry, that's where they are." He stands and walks across the floor to the coffee pot. "I told them all this wasn't a good idea as soon as I found out who Knox was wanting to mess with." He pours a cup and takes it back to the table. "You and your family are a bit of a legend around here, you know?"

"Do you know what Knox wants me to do?"

He looks up at me. "I do. And I also know that he has a backup plan if you fail. Nothing will stop him from getting what he wants."

"Why are you telling me all this?"

"I'm sick of me and my boys being under his thumb. We've paid back our debts to him, but he still thinks he can control us." He rises from his chair and holds out his hand to shake. "I just need someone to put an end to all this."

I shake his hand. "Don't worry. Nothing will stop me from putting an end to him this time."

He nods like he's taking me at my word, and I turn and walk out of the house. The second I'm back on the trail that leads to my bike, I'm calling Brooklyn. The phone only rings once before she answers, sounding breathless.

"John...she's gone. Zoe's gone."

"I know."

"Did you find Jake? Is she with him?"

"They're not here. But I know where they are. I'm heading there now," I say into the phone as I damn near run through the overgrown forest.

"Be careful, John. I love you."

"I love you too." I hang up the phone and slide it back into my pocket, ready to track down Jake and Zoe and put an end to all this shit.

CHAPTER FOURTEEN

Jake

"Oh my God, Zoe, are you okay?" I rush over to her and pull her into my arms, and then I feel the stickiness on her face. I pull back to look at her. "I will fucking kill them!" I run to the door and beat on it with my fists. "You fucking cowards! I'll kill you for touching her!"

"Jake, I'm okay," she says, wrapping her arms around my waist, trying to calm me down. "I've been so scared. Are you okay?"

I turn in her arms to hold her. "I'm fine, but they are not going to be when all this is over." I brush her blonde hair that is stained with her blood out of her face and kiss her lips. "Are you sure you're all right?"

"I think so. I was having some sharp pains in my belly earlier, but they've stopped."

I take her hand and pull her over to the small two-seater, beat-up sofa and sit down beside her. "How did they get you?"

"I went to the house to pick up some papers, and they were inside. I shot one of them in the foot, and the other one was too strong for me to fight, and I didn't want to hurt the baby." She starts crying.

"Shhh...it's okay. I'm going to get us out of here one way or another."

She digs in her pocket and places something in my hand. "This is the only thing I could find to use as a weapon."

"Good thinking. The bolt is long enough that it could do some damage."

"Have you been kept here the whole time?" She looks around the room as she brushes the tears from her pink cheeks.

"No, they moved me. I think they suspected that I got word to John about where to find me and they changed locations. I'm not sure if I'm on the same island or not, but I think this place will be easier to break out of. All the windows have been boarded up, and at least I'm not behind a steel cage anymore."

Her tears start to flow harder. "I've never been so scared. I thought I wouldn't see you again."

I kiss the tears streaming down her face and holder her tighter to me. "I'm not missing out on this little one or you. You're my life, and I would kill to get back to you." I pull her into my lap. "I promise that I will die before I let anything happen to you and the baby."

"I want us all home, safe and sound," she says, then winces in pain, holding her stomach.

"Are you having contractions?"

"It's too soon."

"I'm getting you out of here now!" I stand and grip the bolt in my hand. "Stay right here and close your eyes. I don't want you to see what I'm about to do." Walking over to the door, I beat on it with both my fists. "We need help in here!"

I take a step back and get ready when the doorknob turns. As soon as he steps inside, I drag him through the door and put my body against the weight of the door to shut it and grab him around the neck from behind. He drops his gun, and I jab the bolt into his eye. He lets out a piercing scream and bends over, holding his face. I scramble for the gun, and as I dive for it and roll over, he lunges toward me, and I squeeze the trigger. He falls face-first on top of me with a bullet hole to the chest.

The other guy bursts through the door, and I take aim. "Don't shoot," he bellows and throws his gun on the ground.

"Get over there." I point to the far side of the room. He moves slowly with his hands in the air. I get off the ground and take Zoe's hand with my free hand and pull her toward the door while keeping aim on him. "Throw me the keys to your car," I tell him.

He tosses them. "It won't start."

"Don't come after us or I will kill you too." I drag Zoe through the door and shut it behind us. "You can open your eyes now."

She does but bends over in pain. "The pain is getting worse, Jake."

I pick her up in my arms and carry her to the car, laying her in the back seat. I climb in the driver's side and put the keys in the ignition, but it doesn't turn over. "Fuck!" I yell and get out and open the hood of the car. I glance over at the rundown house, and the guy is looking out the front door. I take aim with the gun and shoot it in his direction, hitting the door as he slams it shut.

I look under the hood of the car quickly to figure out why it won't start and fix a couple of the wires. I get back inside, and it starts up. Zoe lets out a scream as the engine turns over.

"The baby kicked me hard!" Fear is radiating from her.

"It's okay, baby. I'm getting us out of here." Placing my arm on the back of the seat, I put the car in reverse, sending dirt and dust flying into the air. When I get to where I can turn the car around, I see the guy come out of the house aiming a gun at us. I throw it in drive but feel the *pop* of the tire as he shoots.

"Keep your head down," I tell Zoe and take off. The car bounces out of control with the flat tire on the dirt road. As I round a corner, I catch sight of a motorcycle just in time to serve out of the way. It sends us bouncing into a ditch, straight into a tree. The airbag flies out and slams into my face, dazing me.

I come around when Zoe cries out in pain again. Someone is opening the back door, and I scramble out of the car sweeping my gun toward whoever it is.

"It's me, Jake. Don't shoot." John's hands go in the air.

I lower my gun and shake the fog from my head and so relieved to see my brother's face. "Zoe's in labor. We have to get her to the hospital."

We both hear the click of the gun. "Don't fucking move." The guy from the house has his gun pointed at my head. "Drop your gun."

I look at John, hoping like hell he has his. He glances over to the motorcycle, and I see his black duffel bag and know we are screwed.

My captor keeps the gun aimed at me and opens the back door. "Get out of the car," he tells Zoe. She crawls out, and he yanks her into his side. "I said drop the fucking gun!"

"Okay, man. Don't hurt her." I toss the gun in the bushes. "She's in labor and needs to go to the hospital." I keep my hands in the air.

"That's not my problem," he snarls.

"It will be your problem if the baby dies," John says. "Knox didn't instruct you to kill anyone, especially an innocent child."

He bends his neck to the side, cracking it. "Well, if you would have done what he told you to do, she wouldn't have been taken."

John steps around to the back of the car with his hands in the air. "Let her go, and you can keep me."

The man chuckles. "No way in hell do I want to keep you prisoner. I've heard stories about you."

"Then keep me and let him take her to the hospital."

"No," Zoe cries out.

"You still have a job to finish," he tells John.

"I'll take her to the hospital, and then I'll free Knox, but you need her alive. Brooklyn needs her to help with the cure that Knox is looking for."

He contemplates what John is saying to him. He walks with Zoe over to John's motorcycle. He keeps the gun aimed at her and takes John's bag off the bike. "You"—he waves his gun at John—"take off your belt and strap his hands behind his back."

John hesitates. "Just do as he says," I tell him. He removes his belt, and I place my hands behind my back.

"It better be tight," he snarls again.

Once he's done, he tells John to step back. He walks toward me with Zoe and shoves her at John while grabbing hold of my arm. "Get her out of here, and I'll be in touch with Knox to make sure you're doing your job. If not, you can kiss this one goodbye."

"If you hurt him, I will hunt you down and slowly kill you." It's the first time in a long time I see the killer in John's eyes.

"Just take care of her and make sure the baby is okay," I tell him.

He pulls me away, but I keep looking back to see Zoe. John is helping her straddle the motorcycle. I watch until I hear the roar of his bike, and he takes off with Zoe's arms wrapped around his waist.

He shoves me all the way back to the little house, pushing me inside. I trip over the other man's body and land beside him. His eyes are fixed, and there is a puddle of blood pooling around his body. My stomach rolls, knowing that I killed a man.

"You're lucky I need you alive, or you would be dead right alongside him." He kicks me in the side and then goes outside.

I lie on the floor with my hands bound behind me. All I can do is think about Zoe and hope like hell John can get her to the hospital in time.

CHAPTER FIFTEEN

John

I'm sitting at Zoe's side, one hand in hers and the other covering my eyes so the doctor can check the progress of her labor. I would've loved to be out in the hallway for this, but she wouldn't let go of my hand. I have to be here for her any way I can, so here I sit, hoping and praying that I don't see or hear anything I shouldn't.

"Okay, Zoe," the doctor says. "John, you may open your eyes now. She's all covered."

I remove my hand slowly, peeking in small amounts just to be sure he's not trying to trick me. Once I see the blanket at the foot of the bed, I remove my hand completely and sit upright instead of being scrunched down in the chair.

"It looks like you are in the very early stages of labor."

"What? No, I can't be going into labor yet. Jake isn't here!"

The doctor holds up his hand. "This could take hours or even days. I suggest you go home and relax. When your contractions are closer together or your water breaks, come back."

She takes a deep breath and nods before the doctor leaves the room. "What are we going to do, John? We have to get Jake out of there."

I look over at her and brush a stray hair from her face. "I will. I'm going to take you back to my house so Brooklyn can keep an eye on you, and then go after Jake. I have to hurry before they try moving him again."

She nods as she sits up, swinging her legs over the side of the bed. "Hand me my clothes.

I turn and grab her clothes off the table and pass them to her. "I'll be outside when you're done."

I make my way into the hallway and pace back and forth while waiting for her. Somewhere in the middle of my pacing and being lost in my thoughts, a nurse's voice pulls me away.

"Can you believe that? Now tell me, why would they put such a dangerous man in a minimum-security prison. Someone had to know he would bust out eventually."

My pacing stops, and I turn toward her voice. I take a few steps in her direction to find her in a patient's room, standing in front of the TV.

Without thinking, I walk into the room and turn to look up at the TV to see the words, *jailbreak*, scrolling on the screen over and over. The announcer is going on about not picking up any hitchhikers, but I can't tear my eyes away from the screen. The images are flashing from the police, to the guards, to the prisoners all behind bars while they cheer for their fellow inmate.

"Who broke out?" I ask the nurse, still not averting my eyes from the TV.

"That big pharmaceutical bigwig, Knox," she answers. "Hey, don't I know you? You're the one that led to his arrest, aren't you?"

I don't answer her. I spin around and head for the door, nearly bumping into Zoe. "Are you ready?"

"Yeah, I just need my discharge papers."

I take her arm and lead her down the hall. "No time for that."

"What's going on, John?" she asks once we're in the elevator.

"Nothing for you to worry about. I'm just in a hurry to get to Jake."

It doesn't take long before I'm leading Zoe through the house. I sit her down on the couch and walk into the kitchen to find Brooklyn pouring a cup of coffee. She spins around to face me, and I immediately notice the dark circles around her eyes. She's been working too hard and not getting any sleep.

"John! Did you find Jake and Zoe?" she asks, rushing into my arms.

"Zoe's in the early stages of labor. She's on the couch resting."

"And Jake?"

I shake my head and walk her a few more steps into the kitchen, so Zoe doesn't overhear what I'm about to tell her. "They still have Jake." I place my hands on her biceps and level my eyes on her. "Knox broke out."

"What?" she asks, covering her mouth with her hand.

"I had to take Zoe to the hospital, and I saw it on the TV. That means he's coming here for the cure."

"But...but it's not ready!"

I pull her against my chest and hug her to calm her nerves. "I'm afraid he will have no use for Jake anymore. I have to get to him before he's killed."

"What? This is what you've been keeping from me since we left the hospital?" Zoe says, rushing to my side.

Damn it. I didn't want her worried any more than she already is. I turn to face her but keep Brooklyn at my side. "It's okay, Zoe. Knox just got out. It will take him some time to get here. I can get Jake and be back before he arrives."

She's shaking her head while tears flow freely from her eyes. "If he's out, what if he's already had him killed?" Her legs give out, but Brooklyn and I each catch an arm before she hits the floor.

I help her back to the living room. Just as she sits down on the couch, she grabs her stomach and calls out.

I turn around to face Brooklyn. "I need you to keep an eye on her. Time her contractions. If they get closer together or her water breaks, get her to a hospital even if I'm not back with Jake. Got it?"

She nods and follows me to the door. "John!" she calls out, stopping me.

I stop and to see her come running up to me. Her arms are wrapped around my neck, and her lips are against mine. "Be careful. I love you."

"I love you too. Make sure all the doors and windows are locked. Don't let anyone in while I'm gone." I lean in, press one more kiss to her lips and walk out the door.

I stop by my shop and load up with guns and ammo since I lost all mine. I'm going to kill the guy, save my brother, and get my guns back.

After I have a handgun strapped to my body and another riffle on the bike, I'm taking back off to save my brother. Nothing will stop me this time. I feel like a dumbass for being caught off guard to begin with. Running into them like that took me by surprise. I wasn't expecting to crash into them, nor was I expecting Zoe to be in labor. I admire Jake for what he did; I would've done the same thing, but now it's time to get him out of there. I missed L.J. being born, no way will I let him miss out on an experience like that. All I hope is that he's still alive and in the same place. There is no time to waste.

CHAPTER SIXTEEN
Brooklyn

"Zoe, lay down and take a nap. I need to go back to the lab. I feel like I'm so close to the cure, but I'm having a hard time staying focused with everyone's lives in danger."

"Let me go with you. I can help." She gets up off the couch, holding her lower belly.

"I don't think that's such a good idea."

"I'm not going to be able to rest knowing that our men are still out there. Jake looked so tired, and I know this ordeal will change him forever." She looks down toward her feet.

"Jake is tough. He'll be fine." I run my hand down her arm.

"He killed a man today. I know when he stops to think about what he did, it will weigh heavy on him."

"Jake did what he had to do to get you out of there. He would do it a million times over if it meant saving your life. Jake has been through hell and back with us. He's a survivor."

"I know you're right. I've just never seen him angry much less in an all-out protective mode."

I take her by the hand. "Come on. Let's get you cleaned up a bit. Maybe a warm shower will settle you down enough to rest."

She follows me up the stairs. "I think a shower is a great idea. I'd love to get this caked-on blood out of my hair."

"Take as long as you need. I'm going to go back downstairs and put on a kettle of your favorite green tea." She goes into the master bathroom, and I shut the door behind her. I know I need to get to the lab, but I can't leave her. I'm going to have to take her with me.

After setting the kettle on the stove, I lean against the counter and bite at my nails. I'm missing something in the process for the cure. Maybe I need to turn up the hertz to cause the plaque to disintegrate. The sound vibrations need to be stronger. I can refigure my calibrations to increase the intensity.

The kettle whistle gets my attention. Placing the tea bags in each mug, I pour the steaming hot water into each cup. I place them on a bamboo tray along with some cheese and crackers and head up the stairs. When I walk into the room, Zoe is sitting on the edge of the bed with a towel wrapped around her and one covering her hair.

"I don't have any clothes over here to change into," she says, squeezing the ends of her hair with the towel.

"I'll get you a pair of John's sweatpants and a T-shirt." I place the tray on the bed beside her and rummage through John's dresser drawers. "These will work until we can run by your house for you to change."

"I'll be glad when I can wear my own clothes again." She laughs, taking the clothes from me.

"I remember that feeling well. I didn't think after Jack that I would ever be able to fit back into my clothes. It seemed so much harder." I take a mug and sit next to her. "I think with L.J., I was so stressed, the weight fell off me, but with Jack, I was fat and happy." I take a sip of my tea.

She leans her wet head on my shoulder. "I'm so glad you had Jake when L.J. was born."

"I don't know what I would have done without him. I'm glad he has you now. He deserves to be happy. Go get dressed so we can go to the lab and put our heads together and I can keep an eye on your contractions."

"They were a little more intense when I was under the warm water, but they aren't as bad now." She gets up and goes into the bathroom to get dressed.

I hear the chirping the front door makes when it's being opened. I glance down at my watch; John hasn't been gone that long to be back already. I tiptoe to the bedroom door and quietly close it, locking it shut. I pat the pocket of my jeans. "Damn it." My cell phone is downstairs. I rush over to John's side of the bed and pull on the drawer of the bedside table. John always keeps a gun close by, but it's locked because of the kids. I feel around for a key but can't find it.

"What are you doing," Zoe says when she sees me on all fours.

I raise my finger to my lips. "There's someone in the house," I say in a hushed voice.

"Maybe Jake escaped." She throws down the towel and heads for the door.

"Zoe, no!" Before I can stop her, she unlocks the door, and it comes crashing open, pushing her against the wall.

"Well, well, look who I found," Knox says, pointing his men toward me.

I scramble to my feet to be at Zoe's side. "Get away from her!" I scream.

His men yank us apart and tie our hands behind our backs. Knox stands only steps from me. He reaches out and brushes my hair back out of my face. "God, no wonder John fought so hard to get back to you. You get more beautiful as the years have passed."

"And you're still an ugly bastard," I snarl.

He has a sick smile on his aged face. He reaches toward me again, and I latch onto his hand with my teeth. He screams out in pain as I feel his flesh tear from his skin as he pulls away. He strikes out with his other hand, slapping me across the face. "You bitch!" he yells as I fall back against the wall. One of his men snatches the towel off the floor and wraps it around Knox's hand. I watch as his blood soaks through.

"I should have known John would never be married to a woman that wasn't a fighter like him," he growls. Grabbing me hard by the arm, he pulls me to my feet. "You are going to give me what I want, or I'm going to kill her and the baby right in front of you."

"John will be back any minute." I say it so hard, spit flies in his face.

"I waited and watched him leave. With the amount of weapons he was loading, I'm sure he's going after your brother-in-law. My men will stop him before he even gets to his brother."

"No!" Zoe shrieks, but I'm not sure if it's from his words or if she's in pain.

"She's in labor, Knox. Let her go, and I will willingly go with you."

"She is not going anywhere." His men drag us to the door and down the stairs.

"You know John will never be caught by your men again. If you hurt either one of us, it won't matter what cure you have. He will kill you with his bare hands."

"If you don't give me the cure, your children will be orphans! Now shut your damn mouth and tell us where your lab is!"

"You're a man of many means, and you don't know where the lab is?" I snicker. I know I shouldn't taunt him, but hate is brewing in my gut for this man.

He is almost nose to nose with me. He starts to point his finger in my face but thinks better of it. His expressions are seething to the point his face is turning red. He takes a step back, reining in his temper. "You will not open your mouth again other than to tell me the location of your lab." He cuts his eyes in Zoe's direction, and one of his bulky men pulls her head back by her hair, causing her to yelp.

"Okay. I'll take you there, but you have to promise not to hurt her."

He grits his teeth, and I see a slight nod of his head. I give him the address, and he puts us both in the back seat of his black SUV. One of his men gets in the back with us and keeps a gun pointed at us at all times. Knox gets in the passenger seat and plugs in the address of the lab into his GPS that is displayed on the dash.

"Are you all right?" I whisper to Zoe.

"My contractions are getting stronger," she says, biting her lip. She has a sheen of sweat forming on her forehead.

"I will give him what he wants and get you to the hospital."

"You don't have the cure," she whispers.

"He doesn't know that."

CHAPTER SEVENTEEN
John

I ride back over to the property as quickly as I can. Knowing Knox is out, and is probably on his way, I didn't want to leave Brooklyn. But with Zoe in labor, I have to get to Jake now more than ever.

I've already tried the sneak-up approach, so this time, I ride the bike right up to the front door. No element of surprise here. I'm tired of fucking around. I cut the engine and just as I'm swinging my leg over my bike, two men barrel out of the door, guns aimed. I jump and roll to hide behind the black SUV that's parked in front of my bike while pulling my gun out from my waistband. I get down on my knees and peek under the vehicle. I see their feet, and they are running around the vehicle in opposite directions to better their chances. I shoot one in the ankle, causing him to fall, just as the other man rounds the front of the car. I shoot him in the head; he falls lifeless to the ground.

The other man, he's lying on the dirt, screaming in pain and holding his ankle. I walk around the vehicle and point my gun at his head. "Where's my brother?"

"He's inside!" he yells.

"Give me the key."

"Fuck you," he spits out.

I cock the gun, causing the bullet to fall into the chamber. The sound is enough to put anyone on edge, especially if the gun is being pointed right at your face.

His eyes grow wide, and he starts digging around in his pockets for the keys. He pulls them out and holds them in the air. I grab them and slide them into my pocket. "Let's go," I say, pulling him up by this shirt.

"Where?" he asks, hobbling on one foot.

"You really think I'm going to leave you out here alone to call for backup?" I push him through the gravel. "Now, take me to my brother before you end up like your partner out there."

He leads me through the house and back to the cell Jake's being held in. I unlock the door and shove the man through it, causing Jake to turn in our direction. "John! What are you doing here? Where's Zoe?" He rushes toward me.

"She's at home. Let's get you out of here. I'll explain everything later."

The man I pushed into the cell rolls over on the floor to look at me. "Don't leave me here. I'll die."

"Should've thought of that before you decided to work with a known felon." I close the door and lock it, dropping the key on the floor so if the bastard is lucky enough to have someone come here looking, maybe they can save his ass before he dies.

I lead Jake outside, and we both hop on my bike.

"You do that?" he asks, pointing to the man on the ground.

"I didn't have a choice," I say, kicking the bike to life.

Without another word, I shift into first gear and twist the throttle, giving enough gas to soar through the air at record speed. The bike is loud, being pushed to top speed, and the air in our ears is so loud we can't talk on the ride back. I'm sure Jake is wondering why I'm driving so recklessly, but I have to get back home before Knox shows up to find the girls alone.

We pull up a while later, and the second we stop, I cut the engine. Jake is in just as big of a hurry as I am. He's off the bike and rushing toward the front door. I put down the kickstand and run to the house. How'd he get in? That door was locked. Knox has already been here. I run through the house, yelling Brook's name, but there's no answer. I meet back up with Jake in the living room.

"They're gone, man. Where'd they go? Do you think Brook took her to the hospital?"

My eyes fall on the TV where I see a news broadcast. The words, *prisoner escaped and could be in area,* scrolls across the screen. "I don't think so." I nod toward the screen.

Jake pushes past me to watch the TV. "Knox is free?"

"He knew I'd never do it. He had a backup plan. And now he's coming for the cure. Come on. We need to check out the lab."

We both run back out the door and jump on the bike. I'm about to push the button when I finally realize that we no longer need to be on the same bike. I look over my shoulder. "Get your own bike. Both our asses on one is slowing us down!"

"Right, sorry," he says, jumping back off and running toward the garage.

While I wait, I pull out my phone and call Brooklyn's and Zoe's phones. They both go straight to voicemail. I'm sliding the phone back into my pocket when I hear the roar of the bike and the garage door open. I kick my bike to life and shift into gear just as Jake's pulling up to my side.

"Let's go." We both twist the throttle and shoot through the air, heading for the lab.

I lead us to the lab and stop a few hundred feet away, to scope out the place. The building is quiet, but there is a strange black Hummer parked out front. The windows are so dark I can't make out if someone is inside or not.

"What are we waiting for?" Jake asks, coming up behind me to peek at the building.

"We can't just walk in there. We need a plan."

"The fuck we do. Zoe is in there, and she's in labor." He takes a step forward, but I stop him by putting my hand on his chest.

"Knox isn't going to kill them. Brooklyn doesn't have the cure as far as I know. If he kills her, he'll never get it."

"Yeah, if he kills *her*. What's stopping him from killing Zoe? I'm going in there, man, whether you like it or not." He pushes past me, heading toward the lab.

"Fuck," I mumble under my breath as I chase after him.

I'm checking out the surroundings as we draw closer to the building, but I don't see anyone on guard. That's strange. Knox should know better.

There are no windows in the building, and there are only two exits — one in the front and one in the back. Brooklyn only uses the back to keep from being seen as much as possible. The front is always locked, so I direct him to the back.

The door is made up of metal; no window is in the door. There's no way to get a visual inside the building. I put my ear to the door, hoping to detect who all is in there.

"This is ridiculous, man. Just go in. They might not even be here." Jake pushes my shoulder, trying to get me to move.

I stand up straight when I hear, "Freeze."

Slowly, we turn around, and we're face to face with the two men holding guns at our heads.

My anger makes my blood boil. I knew he had to have someone on watch. If Jake hadn't been in such a hurry, I would have found them and taken them out before they even saw me.

"Hand over your weapons," one of the men says.

I grind my teeth together as I dig around my body, handing over every last gun I have hidden. While one man holds the gun on us, the other searches us with a quick pat down. When he's happy that we have nothing, he pushes us inside.

"Look who we found."

Brooklyn, Zoe, and Knox all look up.

"Jake," Zoe says, breathing out from her position in the desk chair. She's holding her stomach and breathing heavily. I can tell labor is getting closer.

"Brook." I rush toward her and pull her against my chest. "Are you okay?"

"I'm fine, John. Are you okay?"

I nod, not taking my eyes off Knox who's standing there, watching us like we're his favorite TV drama.

He smiles wide. "Now that we're all caught up, why don't you come over here with me, John, and let Brooklyn get back to work."

I look at her. "Did you figure out the cure?"

"I'm close," she says, but there is something in her eyes that I don't understand.

"John, now," Knox says from behind me.

I press a kiss to her forehead and release her to get to work as I walk back over to Knox. The second I'm close, one of the guards draws his weapon and aims it at me.

Knox holds up his hand, silently telling him to lower the weapon.

"How'd you get out?" I ask.

He shrugs and laughs. "I'm a pretty important guy. I have my ways...no thanks to you."

I shake my head as my jaw twitches with anger. "You knew I'd never do it, didn't you?"

He lets out a menacing chuckle. "You played your part just like I knew you would. I knew you'd leave your wife alone to save your brother. What I wasn't expecting was this." He motions toward Zoe. "Her being in labor is a problem. She's hampering my progress. I should kill her and the little brat she's carrying."

I step toward him with my teeth bared but retreat when I hear the sound of a bullet fall into the chamber.

Knox snorts. "Take it easy, John. As soon as this gorgeous wife of yours has what I need, we'll be out of your hair."

"It's not that simple!" Brooklyn yells from behind her lab equipment.

"You better hope you get it figured out and soon. I'm a wanted man. I need my cure so I can leave the country and disappear forever." He looks at me. "Just think, this could be the last time we see one another. Makes this meeting a little bittersweet, doesn't it?"

"The only thing stopping me from killing you once and for all is the fact that my dumbass brother rushed in here half-cocked. I would've had your men killed by now, and I'd be coming for you."

He opens his mouth to reply, but Zoe lets out a scream that gets all of our attention.

"Better hurry, Brooklyn. It seems we're running out of time."

Brook looks up from her work. "What is it that you want from me? You expect me to put this cure together in a rush just because I have a gun on me? I haven't been able to figure it out, and I've been working on it for years!"

He trains his eyes on her but doesn't talk.

"Are you really going to inject something that hasn't been tested into your body. It could kill you immediately. These things take time!" she says, sternly.

Knox pulls his gun from his waistband and aims it at her while taking a step forward. "Time isn't something we have!"

"Hey." I jump in front of the gun, more than willing to take a bullet so Brooklyn doesn't have to.

Zoe lets out another painful scream.

"I think the baby is coming. Her contractions are getting closer together," Jake says, looking at his watch.

I look at Knox. "She needs to go to a hospital...unless you want to be the one to deliver the baby."

"No! Nobody leaves." He waves the gun around at each of us.

I hear a gasp and turn around to see a confused look covering Jake's face.

"My water just broke. This baby is coming now," Zoe says.

I look back at Knox. "I hope you took some medical classes while you were in prison because it looks like you'll be delivering a baby."

He aims the gun at Brooklyn. "She can do it."

I look over my shoulder at her and back. "If she does it, that's time wasted on finding your cure. She needs to go to the hospital," I try again.

"Fuck!" Knox screams, pacing the floor.

We all stand around and wait for him to make his decision. "Fine."

Jake helps Zoe stand and moves slowly to the door.

"But not you." He points at Jake, and they stop.

"What? She's having my baby!" Jake is seething mad.

Knox shakes his head. "No." He looks at me. "You take her."

"Me?" I ask, confused.

He nods. "You want her to go so bad, you take her."

I try to argue, but he stops me. "You see, if this all falls apart, I'm going to kill Brooklyn and Jake, ruining two families — not just one."

CHAPTER EIGHTEEN

Jake

I release Zoe and charge after Knox, only to be grabbed by the shirt collar from John, mere inches from Knox's gun. "You son of a bitch! I'm going with her! You will have to kill me to stop me!"

Gunfire pierces my eardrums as I feel the whoosh of the bullet shoot past my head, crunching into the wall behind me. "I'm growing tired of you not doing what you are told. You have been a pain in the ass since you were captured. I have no fucking problem killing you!" he snarls and points the gun in my face.

"Jake, it's okay, please just do as he says," Zoe cries.

I've never in my life wanted to kill someone with my own bare hands before, but right now, I can envision my fingers gripped around his throat, pressing into his fleshy skin, closing off his airway. Watching as his last breath leaves his evil body.

"I've seen that same look in your eyes before from John." He laughs.

"Make no mistake," I say, "I will be the one to kill you."

John steps in between us and faces me. "Don't taunt him. I will take care of Zoe. You make sure Brooklyn stays safe," he says with his voice lowered as he is slowly moving me backward away from Knox. He mouths the words, "kill him," and walks past me, wrapping his arm around Zoe's waist to help her walk out the door.

"Wait," I yell. I glare at Knox and walk over to Zoe. "I love you, baby." I place my hand on her belly. "I love this baby, too. I'll get there as soon as I can, I promise."

"Just don't get yourself killed," she says. "We both need you."

"If she's not out of here on the count of three, I may change my mind about letting her go at all." Knox waves his gun around. One of his goons opens the door and follows them out, leaving only one behind with him. He's the size of a brick wall, and I'm not sure how I'm going to take him out, but I will. I have a moment of feeling completely helpless as the door closes behind Zoe and John, then a determination like I've never felt fills me. I bump Knox's shoulder as I walk past him to stand next to Brook.

"What can I do to help?"

"Put some gloves on." She motions to a box of gloves sitting on a small square metal table. Once I have them on, she hands me two vials. One is filled with a blue-colored liquid, the other one with tiny silver-looking beads. "Mix these two together when I tell you and then pour it into here." She points at a small open port in one of the machines.

She walks around to the other side of the room and starts pressing buttons on one of the panels of the ultrasound machine. Then she walks back over to what looks like a computer screen but is filled with a black-and-white X-ray of a human skull. The vessels are all highlighted in white. You can actually see the pulsating of the arteries as blood moves through them. There is one area in the middle of a vessel that is completely blacked out.

"What's this," I ask as I put both vials in one hand and look at the screen.

"This is a simulator of a brain filled with plaque and torturous vessels that are believed to cause Alzheimer's. See this vessel below the dark area that is twisted?"

I nod and feel Knox come stand behind me.

"It's my theory that if I can get this to straighten out, the serum that I've created will dissolve the plaque rather than pushing it somewhere else. The tricky part is getting this area untangled."

"Is that what I'm holding?" I hold out the vials.

"Yes, but the tiny little beads are tracers. Without them, I can't watch to see what it does on the screen. When they are injected into the port, they will light up the screen in green, and I can see the effect they will have on the vessels."

"Kind of like injecting a dye into the vessels," I say.

"Exactly." She hands me a large syringe. "Once you've combined them, draw them up into this. This end will fit directly into the port and when I tell you to go, push hard until every drop is inside. Got it?"

I look over my shoulder. "Do you mind giving me some room?" I nudge Knox with my elbow.

He takes one step back. "If you touch me again, I will kill you."

I start to turn toward him, and Brooklyn stops me. "You can't help me if you're dead, Jake."

It takes everything in me to turn away from him. "Tell me when you're ready."

She taps the keys on the computer and walks back over to the ultrasound machine and turns a few knobs, causing the machine to hum. "Mix them together," she says.

I pour the tiny beads into the blue liquid and swirl it around. I take the syringe and place it into the mixture and draw it up until it is all inside of it. I hold it up, showing it to Brooklyn. I glance over my shoulder, and Knox smirks at me. I don't know if it would kill him, but I'd love to force feed him what's inside the syringe.

"Get ready," Brook says.

I line up the syringe in the port and wait.

"Now, Jake." She points at me. I push hard, letting the thick mixture flow into the port, then I step back and watch the screen. Sure enough, you can see it flow through the vessels. It accumulates at the tangled spot. Brooklyn joins me at the screen as she is nervously biting her bottom lip.

"It stopped moving," I say.

"Just wait, give it a minute."

Swirls of motion cover the area below the tangled mess. The vessel looks like it starts to vibrate and slowly uncurls, sending a rush of green to the blackened area. Bit by bit, the black area fades and the green rushes through the rest of the brain.

A big smile covers Brooklyn's face. "What just happened," I ask her.

"It worked. It really worked," she says and grabs me into a hug as she bounces up and down.

"You figured out the cure?"

"Well, it still needs to be tested on humans, but, yes, it looks like I've found the cure."

Her moment of happiness grows quiet as Knox comes into her line of sight. "I knew I could count on you to find the cure for me."

She lets go of me and faces him. "I didn't do it for you, you bastard. If I had my way, you would never get your hands on it. I would enjoy seeing you slowly lose your mind."

He steps close to her and reaches out with his left hand and runs his fingers along her jawline. Her jaw clenches when he makes contact with her skin. "You and I in another lifetime would have made great partners."

I lose my fucking mind and yank his arm upward, causing his gun to fire into the ceiling. I bolt forward, knocking Brook backward and sending Knox against the wall. His wall-sized friend grabs me by the back of the collar, pulling me off Knox. He finagles his arm around my neck, holding me in place. Knox straightens his shirt and pulls his sleeves back down in place.

"I think you are even more difficult than your noto-rious brother is to deal with. Take him to the vehicle and make sure he doesn't cause any more problems. I'll deal with him once Brooklyn here gives me what I want." I watch as he walks over to her. "Maybe I'll even take more than what I've asked for." He looks her up and down.

Now, there is no doubt in my mind that I will kill him. I squirm, and his hold gets tighter around my neck. "Don't you lay a fucking hand on her!"

He laughs and faces me. "Or what, you're going to kill me?"

"Even if you kill me, John will rip you apart limb by limb."

I see fear flash through his face, and then he waves at his man to take me outside. He forces me through the door as I struggle against him.

"You can do this willingly, or I can choke you to death right here," he snarls and applies pressure into my carotid artery.

I give in, knowing if I'm passed out, I can't escape and help Brooklyn. When I quit fighting him, he shoves me into the back seat of the SUV, but not before slamming my forehead against the outside of the door. A rush of blood gushes down my face as I slide into the middle of the seat. I press the palm of my hand into the gash to stop the bleeding. The door slams shut and locks. I try to open the opposite side, but the handle lifts without opening the door.

The front door opens, and he gets inside, slamming the driver's side shut. He turns in his seat and sticks a gun in my face. "Don't try anything," he says with a sick smile on his face. "I won't bat an eye at killing you."

He turns back around and puts black earphones in his ear. I look around the back seat that is completely empty. Even the seatbelts have been removed. There is nothing I can use to escape. I lean back against the seat and watch as his head starts to rock with the music he's listening to. I slowly lean forward, then snatch the cord to the earphones up around his neck, hoping like hell they won't break. I grip them tight in one hand and yank his head backward. His large hands scratch at this neck, trying to free the cord that is biting into his skin and eating away his air. I keep a good grip in one hand and reach forward for the gun that is sitting in his lap.

One of his hands grabs mine as I grasp the gun. I manage to get my finger on the trigger and squeeze, shattering the windshield. He leans forward and strikes me with his elbow, forcing me backward. My grip loosens, and he's climbing over the back of the seat to get to me.

It takes me a second to realize the gun is still in my hand. I raise it up and pull the trigger. My ears ring out in protest, and he collapses onto the seat with his head dangling in my lap. Warm blood covers my thigh before I can push him off me.

Climbing over his dead body, I get in the front seat and open the door. I have no plan or any other thought other than it's time to take out Knox.

CHAPTER NINETEEN
John

I help Zoe into the back seat while Knox's goon climbs behind the wheel. I slide in beside her, and she grabs my thigh, digging her claws in. I let out a yell, and her head jerks up. Her eyes lock on mine, and I swear I can see the pits of hell in them.

"I'm about to squeeze a baby the size of a water-melon out of my vagina, and you can't handle a few fingernails?" She's breathing heavily with her contraction.

"I'm fine," I say, removing her hand from my thigh and holding it in mine. "Just squeeze my hand as hard as you can."

She pulls her eyes away from mine but nods as she breathes through the pain. I hear the man in the front seat snicker as he turns over the engine and shifts into drive.

"What are you laughing at up there? I'll trade you places." I wouldn't ever let him touch Zoe, but it seems like a good threat.

"Nope, I'm just fine where I am," he replies.

Zoe lets out a scream that fills the car, making the driver jerk the wheel and causing my ears to ring with pain.

"Fuck, Zoe. Are you okay? You about busted my eardrum." I place the tip of my index finger into my ear and wiggle it, trying to make the ringing stop.

"John, I swear to God, I'm going to rip off your favorite part if you don't help keep my mind off the pain," she threatens.

"Okay, okay." I'm in full-on panic mode now. I don't remember Brooklyn being this violent when she was having Jack.

I pull my wallet out of my back pocket and open it to show her some pictures. "Here look at this." It's a picture of Brooklyn and the kids sitting on the grass in the backyard.

She smacks the wallet from my hand. "I love those two kids to death, but I don't need any reminders of children at the moment."

I pick up my wallet and put it away. "I hope Jake can handle you. You're kind of mean, you know that?"

Slowly, she turns and gives me the evil eye again. I immediately apologize.

As another contraction starts up. The grip she has on my hand tightens, grinding my bones together. I want to pull it away, but I don't. She needs me.

I'm not a weak man by any means, but this is not the strength of a normal woman. This is Zoe who is currently possessed by a demon. I'm convinced that she is using every fiber of her being to hurt me in any way she can.

I force myself to stay quiet instead of yelling out like I want to. So to deal with the feeling of my bones shattering, I join in on her Lamaze breathing.

"What the hell are you doing, John?" she asks around labored breaths.

I shake my head. "Helping you breathe."

"You're going to pass out doing that." The hold on my hand starts to release.

"I'm fine. Just concentrate on the baby." I am a little dizzy, so I lean my head against the headrest and try to find my bearings.

Zoe starts rubbing her stomach. "Do you think Jake and Brook will be okay?"

With my hand now free, I massage it, hoping to ease away any pain and bruising that may occur. "Everything will be fine. Jake will take care of Knox, and he will be with you before you know it."

"I hope you're right," she whispers.

We pull up to the hospital, and I throw open the door. Stepping out, I reach out my hand for Zoe to take. She slides across the black leather seat and gets out, holding her swollen stomach. We walk slowly through the entrance doors, and I find a wheelchair for her to sit in. I'm damn near running through the hospital while pushing her in the chair.

"John, you're going to give me whiplash with the way you're running. Slow down!" she yells.

I slow my pace to a light jog instead of a full-on sprint. When we get to the maternity ward, I stop at the counter, but nobody is behind it. I bang on the top with my hand. "Hello? Pregnant lady in labor here!" I yell.

Zoe places her hand on my arm. "John, it's okay. We have time."

"We have time? Your contractions are getting closer and closer together. We don't have much time."

"Yes, we do. Jake's not here yet." I can see the pain etched on her face. It's not labor pains though; it's the pain she feels when she thinks about the father of her child missing being here for this. It fills me with pain because Brooklyn had to go through the same thing when I was locked away.

I kneel down to her level. "Zoe, I know you don't want to hear this, but there is a chance that Jake won't make it. This baby is on its way. There is no stopping it. But I promise that I will be here every step of the way."

Tears fill her eyes, and she nods her head while biting her bottom lip. "I know. I'm just praying that he makes it in time."

"Can I help you?" a nurse asks as she rounds the corner.

I jump up to my feet. "Yes, she's in labor."

The nurse smiles kindly. "How wonderful. Has your water broken yet?"

"Yes, about ten minutes ago." The second she gets the words out, she lets out a scream while holding her stomach.

The nurse jumps into action. She takes Zoe's wheelchair and pushes her down the hallway, into a room.

"Dad, you need to put this on." She hands me a gown.

"I'm not the dad," I say, pulling my arms through the yellow sleeves of the gown.

She helps Zoe up and sets her on the edge of the bed. "I don't care who you are, just get it on and get into position. This baby is coming now." She digs around in a drawer and pulls out another gown. "We need to get this on you, honey."

Zoe nods while breathing heavily. I turn my back while the nurse helps Zoe undress and get into the gown. When I'm told I'm in the clear, I make my way to the side of her bed, sitting down in the empty chair at her side.

"We're going to do a quick check here," the nurse says as she lifts the sheet on Zoe's lower half.

I jump and quickly turn my head to look at her face. Her eyes land on mine, and she giggles. "What's the matter, John? Feeling a little uncomfortable?"

"A little bit," I answer with wide eyes.

"I'm going to get you moved into a birthing room and call the doctor. This baby is coming now." The nurse lowers the blanket back into place before running from the room.

"John, I can't do this," Zoe cries.

"Shhh, you can. It will be okay. I promise, Zoe." I hold her hand and offer any support I can.

She shakes her head. "No, he's not here. He's not going to make it."

I use my free hand to push fallen hair out of her face. "Jake will be fine, and he'll be here as soon as he can. I'll help you with this. I mean, we do look a lot alike," I joke. "Pretend I'm him."

She cries harder. "You don't look anything like him."

"We're twins for God's sake!"

"We're ready to move you now," the nurse says, walking back in with another nurse behind her.

I stand and move out of their way, staying close behind them as they push Zoe's bed out of the room and down the hall.

As I'm following along, I hear nothing but screams — screams from other women in labor and screams from Zoe. I feel like it's judgment day and I'm being led to the gates of hell.

Please hurry up, Jake, I silently pray.

CHAPTER TWENTY
Brooklyn

K nox is hovering too closely for comfort as I frantically write down everything I did in my journal. My skin starts to crawl when I feel his breath on my neck.

"Your brain makes you so enticing. I love a woman with a beautiful mind. John is a very lucky man." His voice oozes with vile intent.

"Don't even think about touching me or you will never get what you want."

He brushes the hair off my shoulder. "Maybe I've changed my mind about what I want from you. I may be willing to lose my mind for a woman like you."

As I stand from my desk chair, I roll it backward, making him move. He pushes the chair out of the way and snatches me by the waist, pulling my body flush with his.

"You are a fucking wildcat." He makes the mistake of putting both of his hands in my hair and pressing his lips to mine because it frees up my hands. I shove him far enough away from me to plant a knee in his groin. He crumples over in pain.

"I told you not to touch me. You're lucky John isn't here, or it would be much more than your balls aching right now."

He coughs out a few times trying to regain his composure. He takes a step toward me, and I hold out a filled syringe in front of me. "You touch me one more time, and you will never get this cure, and neither will anyone else."

He stops, but he laughs. "You would never hold back such a great cure for mankind." He shakes a finger at me while he's smiling. "That's your problem you know. This entire thing, including missing out on your husband for years, is your fault. You have this need to cure the ailments of the world but have never once considered how it would affect you and the people you love. Did you not think people would kill for your knowledge? Or, the people that would lose money because of your knowledge would not try to shut you down? You're trying to save a world that is full of greedy men like myself. If it wasn't me after you, there would be someone else more ruthless."

"Good thing I don't do it for people like you. I do it for the Jakes of the world. He's still alive because of my cure, my hard work, and dedication. Unlike you, he makes the world a better place. He deserves a life free of illness. You deserve nothing but misery."

His face fills with anger as bright red covers his pale skin. "You don't think I've had enough misery in one lifetime?" he yells. "You know nothing about me!"

"I know you've paid to have people killed, including John."

"Your precious John took my money willingly. So what makes him any less evil than me?"

"John has a heart. You don't," I spit out in anger.

He walks away and starts pacing the room. "I had a heart once, and it was ripped out of my chest."

"That's hard to believe," I snort.

"I was a young man madly in love with a brilliant woman, not too much unlike you." He stops his pacing in front of me. "I watched her wither in pain, eaten up from cancer, and there wasn't a damn thing I could do about it."

"So instead of helping spread the cure for cancer and getting the pharmaceutical companies to affordably manage the cure for cancer, you team up with them to keep others from being cancer free?" I'm confused as to why he would do that.

"I'm a sick bastard like that. If she couldn't be cured, I didn't want anyone else to be either. I got rich off these companies, and if she were alive today, I would have the money to get her whatever she needed. Kind of like what I'm doing for myself right now." He nods toward my equipment.

"Don't fool yourself into thinking you're getting any of this because you can afford it. Your goons and their guns are the only reason you're getting anything from me."

"Well, my money affords those goons to get me whatever I want."

"Do you really think this woman you protest to love would have been happy with your choices now?"

He takes the chair in his hands and picks it up, throwing it across the room. "My wife is dead, so it really doesn't matter what she thinks!" He's baring his teeth as he thrusts out his chest. It's the first time I've seen him sweat, and it frightens me.

I raise my hands up in surrender. "Let me finish my paperwork, and then you can walk away with the cure you want." I really have a hard time picturing this man loving anyone, but his reaction suggests that maybe he did have a heart at one time. Picking up my chair off the ground, I place it back in front of my desk and sit. I make a few notes and realize he's standing behind me again.

"Did you and your wife have any children?"

He walks around me and leans his frame on the edge of the desk. "A son."

"Where is he?" I ask, fixing my eyes on his. I see nothing but pain coming back from them.

"He hates me for what I've done." His shoulders hunch as he drops his chin to his chest.

"There is still time to change that."

His moment of vulnerability passes in a flash. "My son is none of your concern. If you don't hurry up, your children are going to be without a mother." He stands, pointing at my journal.

I scribble one last note. "Are you going to take this to your people to have them test the formula?"

"No. I trust that you have formulated it correctly because you have too much to lose if it's not right."

"You never know. I may have created a formula to kill you by changing one little thing."

Before I can move, his hand flies out, hitting me square in the face, jarring me out of my chair and onto the floor. He shoves the journal in his pocket and then tackles me as I try to get up. His hands are around my throat as I try to kick him off me. He keeps one hand firmly around my throat, and with the other, he cups my breast. I buck up, but his weight is too much. I can't get him off me. I let go of his hand around my throat and dig my nails into his cheek. He's like a man possessed and it doesn't even phase him.

I feel the last bit of my breath leaving my body. My eyes blur over, and all I can see is my life—John and the kids.

CHAPTER TWENTY-ONE

Jake

I hear a crash as I make my way back to the lab. Brook is on the floor and Knox is sprawled on top of her, and she's not moving. Rushing over to her, I tackle him to the ground beside Brooklyn. Fists fly as we exchange punches. I get the better hand, and I'm sitting on top of him, choking the life out of him.

He manages to say in a hoarse voice, "By the time you kill me, it will be too late for her." He cuts his eyes toward Brooklyn. I glance over, and she's not breathing. I let go of him and crawl over to her. She has no pulse.

I start CPR. "Goddamn you, Knox!" I say between compressions.

He's gasping for air as he rolls toward me.

I want to kill him, but if I stop, Brooklyn will die. I continue pounding on her chest as he reaches his feet. "She's given me what I need." He pats a book sticking out of his pocket then snatches vials off the lab table.

"Come on, Brook, breathe so I can stop him!"

"Tell John thanks for sharing his wife with me." He laughs.

My anger overtakes my good senses, and I jump off the floor after him. I crash into him, causing the metal table to tip over and make a loud echoing sound in the room. I land on top of him; he rolls over, flipping me off, and my head cracks against the tile floor. I want to vomit on impact. My head spins as I watch as if in slow motion as Knox gets off the ground. He picks up the book that was thrown from his pocket and tucks it back inside. He walks over to the door, turning the knob, but turns around toward me.

"That little stunt you just pulled will cost you your family." He steps outside, leaving the door open behind him.

I stumble to my feet and go back over to Brooklyn. Her eyes blink a few times, and she gasps for breath.

Her hands go to the red fingerprints on her neck.

"You're okay. He's gone," I say, taking her in my arms.

"Jake," she says breathily.

I pick her up and walk outside. All the cars are gone. "Do you think you can stand on your own two feet?"

She nods, and I slowly put her down. "I need to find a phone. Is there one in your lab?"

"My purse is on the table inside. My cell phone is in one of the pockets."

I run back in only to find her purse beneath the table that was toppled over, and her screen is shattered into a hundred little pieces. "Damn it!" I slam my fist on the ground. "We've got to find a way out of here."

"In the shed out back, there is an old motorcycle that I bought John and was going to have it fixed up for him, but I never got around to it with everything that has been going on," she says as she rubs her throat.

I walk back over to her, placing my hands on her shoulders. "Are you okay?" I say, inspecting her neck.

"I'm fine, but we need to get out of here. The keys to the shed are on that shelf." She points to one that is in the corner. I grab them and then take her hand.

"Come on. I'll see if I can get it running." I undo the padlock and pull open the door to the shed. "God, please tell me it runs."

"It started right up for the man I bought it from. It's been sitting in here since it was delivered, so I don't know what it will do."

I put up the kickstand and walk it outside. "This is a beauty, but old," I say as I throw my leg over it. Brook steps inside the shed and comes back out with keys, handing them to me.

I place them in the ignition and push the start button. Nothing happens. I try again, and it makes a sputtering noise and then dead silence.

"Jake, there is a store about a mile up the road. We can call for help from there."

"Just give me a minute," I say, getting off the bike and squatting down in front of the motor. "You wouldn't happen to have any wiring tape?"

She bites at a fingernail. "No, but I think I have something in the lab you can use." She darts off before I can respond, and she's back almost as quickly. "Here, try this."

It's a slim roll of blue tape. I peel up the end and start fastening the loose wires. "That should work," I say, standing.

Brooklyn climbs on this time and turns the key. It sputters, but this time it cranks up. It's a small bike built for one, but we'll have to make it work. "Slide back."

"Any other time I would argue with you," she says as she sits as far back as she can.

I throw my leg over. "You're going to have to hold on tight because I'm going to run this thing as fast as I can." She slides her arms around my waist, and I take off, sending gravel flying behind us. We make it to the asphalt road, and I twist back hard to gain some speed. Smoke is flowing up around us, but I don't let it stop me. I don't even bother slowing down for stoplights, which sends a few cars screeching and horns blowing. I can feel Brook's nails digging into my skin as she's holding on for dear life.

As I round the corner, I see the vehicle that Knox was riding in. I drive up next to him, and I can see the man that I killed slumped over in the seat and

Knox is driving. He sees me and swerves in my direction, causing me to go off on the shoulder of the road. I gain control in enough time to keep us from flying head-on into a ditch.

"Jake, we don't have time to stop him!" Brook screams next to my ear.

"If I don't stop him, he will kill my family." I speed back up and get behind him. I see him watching me in the rearview mirror.

"Just go around him Jake and beat him to the hospital. There is nothing we can do on this bike to slow him down."

I know she's right. I need get to Zoe before he does. I wait until the passing lane is open and I give the bike everything she has. As I'm next to him, he swerves again, but I'm able to keep moving past him by edging over. A truck is headed straight for us. The bike doesn't have anything left to give me as far as speed goes. I make it past Knox's bumper and swing the bike over into his lane as the truck nearly misses us. Knox leans too far right on the steering wheel, and it sends him flying over the shoulder of the road and into a bunch of trees.

I laugh when I look back, seeing Brooklyn shoot him a bird.

There is so much smoke coming out of the bike that we are both choking on the fumes. I slow down, hoping that it won't completely die on us, but no such luck. It spits out some black smoke and stalls. I pull over on the side of the road and Brook jumps off. She has her thumb out trying to hitch a ride. A car blows by her, and her middle finger flies up again.

I hop off the bike and put the kickstand down. "Let's start walking," I tell her.

"Hell with that. We'll never get to the hospital in time." She unbuttons the top two buttons of her blouse.

"What are you doing?"

"Showing some cleavage." She points down at her girls.

"I don't think you've looked in the mirror lately, but we both look rather scary right now." I motion to my beat-up face.

"Speak for yourself. You underestimate the power of these girls," she says, shoving them higher in her bra.

"Okay, Scary Mary, whatever you say." I chuckle and start to hit the pavement.

To my utter surprise, I hear a diesel truck pull over behind me. I turn around, and Brooklyn is standing on her tiptoes with her head poked inside the open window, talking to the driver.

"Come on, Jake," she yells as she's opening the passenger side door. She climbs inside and scoots over on the bench seat, and I slide in next to her.

"I told you. These girls work every time." She winks at me.

"You know the driver, don't you?"

She shrugs and smiles.

CHAPTER TWENTY-TWO

Jake

We have several miles of interstate to drive before we hit the hospital exit, and even though we're driving seventy-five miles per hour, it's still not fast enough for me. All I can hope for is that Zoe hasn't had the baby yet. I'll never forgive myself if I miss the birth of my daughter. I know the guilt missing something like this can cause. I see it every day on John's face.

"Where you two going?" the man behind the wheel asks.

"To the hospital just a few miles up the road," Brooklyn answers.

"Everything okay? Either of you hurt?"

"No, we're fine, Paul. Jake has a baby on the way, and we just happened to be stranded when the bike we were on gave out. You're really saving us here."

"Is that right?" he asks, leaning forward to look at me. "Well, congratulations."

"Thank you." I look at my watch, counting down the minutes until we reach our exit.

Out of the corner of my eye, something flashes in the passenger side mirror. I look up, leaning forward to get a better view in the mirror. I can clearly see Knox behind the wheel of a Ford F-250, and he's coming at us full speed.

"We have trouble," I think out loud.

"What?" Brooklyn asks, turning to look out the back window.

I quickly place my hands on her head and pull it down into my lap while bending down over her. "It's Knox. There's no way he could know we're in this truck unless he sees us."

"Uh, Paul? Would you mind picking up the speed a bit?" Brooklyn asks.

He nods, eyes flashing up to the rearview mirror. "Are you two in some sort of trouble?"

"You could say that." My tone of voice is lifeless, not wanting to admit that we have now brought our trouble into this man's life.

"Don't worry. I'll kick it up a notch." He presses on the gas, causing Brooklyn and me to be thrown back by the force.

After several long seconds of driving faster, I ask, "How's it looking?"

I see his eyes bounce back up to the mirror. "He's right on our trail." He jerks the wheel to the left, throwing us around the cabin of the truck. "He's got a gun!"

"Fuck. He knows we're in here." I sit up and look behind us to see Knox aiming his gun at the truck. I see his windshield shatter, and I duck again, but Paul swerves back into the right-hand lane, causing the bullet to miss us.

"Do you have a gun?" I ask Paul.

"In the glove compartment," he answers.

With Brooklyn's head still in my lap, I open the glove compartment and look into to see a gun resting in its holster. I slide my hand in and pull it out, dropping the holster on the floor and turning the safety off.

Before I can turn around to take aim, Knox fires again, this time causing the back glass to break, but the bullet shoots through the cab and into the dash. If Brooklyn was sitting up, it would have gotten her right in the back.

"Brook, get as low as you can to the floor," I tell her while twisting back again.

She wiggles herself into a ball in the passenger side floorboard, and I get up on my knees in the seat. The back glass is shattered but still attached to the frame. The cracks make it impossible to see through. I use the butt of the gun to hit it with, over and over until slowly it starts falling into the bed of the truck.

With the back glass now gone, wind whips in through the cab with our fast speed, but I can clearly see Knox. I raise the gun, out the back window while using the headrest to block all but my eyes as I aim. It's like slow motion as I squeeze the trigger. The gun practically explodes as the bullet goes flying from the barrel.

All the target practice I've done with John over the years pays off when the bullet hits the spot I was aiming for—the passenger side tire.

The tire explodes and the truck jerks to the right, sending him off the road and right into the guardrail. The impact of the hit causes the front of the truck to crush before it goes flipping over the rail and into the grass where it flips several more times and comes to a stop.

"Stop!" I yell, causing Paul to stomp on the brakes as he jerks the wheel, directing the truck to the side of the road.

When we've come to a complete stop, I throw open my door and jump out. "Stay here," I tell them.

"Wait, Jake!" Brooklyn hops out behind me. "What if he's okay? He has a gun...he will shoot you as soon as he sees you."

I shake my head and hug her quickly. "No way he could have made it through that crash. I just want the peace of mind of knowing for sure that he is out of all of our lives." I press a quick kiss to the top of her head and push her back into the truck. "Wait here," I tell her again.

I slam the door shut and jog back several feet to the crash site. Several people who saw the crash are now pulled over on the side of the road, phones to their ears as they call 9-1-1.

I run past them and drop to my knees at the side of the car, bending down low to see through the busted window. Knox lies lifelessly on the hood of the upturned car.

I *tsk* him. "Should've worn your seat belt."

I can clearly see the blood staining the steering wheel and dash on the driver's side of the car. After an impact like that, I don't know how he wasn't thrown out, but I know he has to be messed up with all the blood.

I grab hold of his ankle and pull him from the car and into the grass. Sure, I could be causing more damage by moving him, but do I really care? Nah, I'm willing to take the chance.

I roll him over to his back and look down on him. His face is so bloody that I don't even recognize him. I place my hand on his wrist and feel for a pulse. It's faint, but it's there.

How in the hell could he survive something like that? I'm half tempted to pull out that gun and shoot him right here and now, but the audience gathering around the side of the road has me thinking otherwise. I don't need to go to prison and miss out on the rest of my daughter's life.

"Fuck," I grumble under my breath.

Before I can make up my mind on whether or not I should leave him or shoot him, my ears are filled with the sounds of sirens.

The police and the EMTs arrive quickly. While they work on getting him on the stretcher, I talk with the police and tell him exactly who is. I'm not taking a chance on him not going back to prison...a maximum-security prison which is exactly where he'll go since he's escaped.

The police thank me for helping to identify him and bring him in, but I have to stop all questions. "Look, I'm more than willing to answer these questions at a later time, but my baby is being born right now. Can you please just follow me to the hospital where we can finish this?"

He nods. "I'll do better than that. I'll give you a police escort." He shakes my hand.

"Thank you," I tell him, shaking his hand and running back to the truck.

I open the door and jump inside. "We're getting a police escort."

"Is Knox..." Brooklyn starts.

"He's alive," I ground out, not happy about it. "But the good thing here is that he's going away for the rest of his life. No more minimum-security prison for him."

The police car pulls out ahead of us, and Paul follows quickly behind. The sirens are blaring loudly as traffic pulls out of the way for us. We're at the hospital in minutes.

The moment the truck stops, I'm throwing open the door and Brooklyn and I are rushing inside, praying we're not too late.

CHAPTER TWENTY-THREE

Jake

"Thank God you are here, man. They just took Zoe to the birthing room." John's hands are on my shoulder, and he looks frantic.

"Why are you out here and not with her?" I growl.

"Because the nurse said she had to get her ready. And, you know..." He lowers his voice. "I didn't want to see her naked."

"For God's sake, John, they don't strip you naked to have a baby." Brooklyn laughs.

"You had all kinds of parts showing when you had Jack. I don't need to see Zoe's bits."

"I don't think Jake was thrilled about seeing me either when I had L.J.," she snorts.

"That's enough about who has seen whose bits. Show me where they took her." I squint my eyes at John.

He points to a set of double doors at the end of the hallway. I move past him and push the doors open to be met with a woman in scrubs raising her voice at me. "You are not allowed back here without scrubs on," she says.

"My wife is back here somewhere," I tell her.

"Here, go in there and put these on and we'll find your wife," she says, opening a changing room door. I don't even bother taking off my clothes; I pull them up and over my jeans and dirty shirt.

"What's your name?" She is scrolling through the computer.

"Jake Remington."

She runs her fingers over the names showing. "I don't have anyone listed under the name Remington?"

"Sorry, we're not married yet. It's Zoe Blake."

She cuts her gaze at me. "She's down the hall, room 205."

I jog past her and find her room on the left. As I open the door, I hear a bloodcurdling scream. Zoe has her legs in stirrups with a blue cloth blanket draped over her. There is a woman gowned up with a white paper hat on, sitting on a stool at Zoe's feet.

"Don't push yet, Zoe," she says.

Zoe's eyes pop open and land on me. "Jake! You made it!" she all but screams with sweat rolling down her face.

Taking her face in my hands, I kiss her all over. "I'm here, baby, I'm here."

"Is he gone?"

"I'll catch you up later. I want you to focus only on the baby."

"With the next contraction, I need you to push, Zoe," the lady at her feet says.

"Jake, this is Dr. Sands."

I automatically hold out my hand to shake and then draw it back. "Sorry. I'm the dad," I say and can't stop the smile that spreads over my face. I place my hand on Zoe's belly for support, and I feel it tightening. Zoe starts her breathing.

"Okay, push with this one," Dr. Sands says.

Zoe leans up, and I support her head and shoulders with my hand, something Brook taught me during her delivery. She bears down and keeps a scream locked behind her teeth. When the contraction finally eases, she lets out an audible moan and relaxes back.

I wipe the hair out of her face and place a soft kiss on her lips. "I want to marry you...today."

"I think I'm a little busy today." She laughs through the tears that are streaming down her face.

"Then as soon as we can. I don't want one more day to go by that you aren't my wife. I love you, Zoe."

Another contraction starts. "You sure as hell better!" She lets out a scream and pushes again.

"Would you like to see the baby crowning?" the doctor asks.

I think about passing out after Brooklyn's baby was delivered. Hell no I don't want to see it. Zoe must have read my mind, and her eyes bore into me. I look over her head and see the ammonia inhalant taped to the wall. Reaching above her, I take it down and hand it to her.

"Hold this, Doc. I might need it." I reluctantly walk and kneel behind the doctor. My face feels warm.

"Breathe, Jake," I hear from Zoe.

I stand up straight and head back over to Zoe. "I've seen enough," I say, trying not to hyperventilate.

"This next push and your baby will be out," the doctor exclaims.

"Are you ready for this?" Zoe asks me.

"More than ready," I tell her and kiss her one last time before her contraction comes on full force.

She's squeezing my hand, and I'm helping her to breathe through it. Then I hear the most beautiful sound—our daughter taking her first breath. The doctor reaches over the blue cover and lays her on Zoe's stomach.

"Do you want to cut the cord, Jake?"

I wave her off with a shake of my head. The doc cuts the cord, and one of the nurses cradles the baby into her arms. "I'm going to check her out, and you can have her right back."

I'm mesmerized by the baby's big blue, round eyes. I follow the nurse to the warm cart she lays my baby in.

I start counting fingers and toes. "They are all there," I yell over to Zoe.

I watch as the nurse wipes down the baby and takes her vitals. "She's beautiful," I say as the nurse swaddles her and hands her to me. When I turn around, Zoe has her arms outstretched.

"Let me see her." She's smiling through her tears. Stepping up next to her, I turn the baby where she can see her as the doctor finishes up working on Zoe. "She has your chin," she says through sobs.

"She has your gorgeous eyes." I plant a gentle kiss on top our daughter's little head.

Handing her over to Zoe, I find a small spot on the bed next to her and sit beside her. "She needs a name."

"I know we had a few picked out, but now that she's here, none of them seem to fit her." She's unwrapping her and checking out every inch of the baby.

"I have an idea for a name," I say, touching her tiny fingers. I place my thumb in her hand, and she grips it.

"What are you thinking?"

"Well, you're changing your name to Remington the minute we get married. How about we name her Blake, so your name stays with her?"

"Blake Remington," she says. "I love it, Jake."

I get down on one knee next to the bed. "Will you marry me today, Zoe?" I ask while kissing the back of her hand.

"Yes. I don't want to wait a minute longer either."

I get off my knee and hold both of my girls close. "I love you both, so much." My own tears drip down and drop on Zoe's shoulder.

She wipes a tear from my face, then gently swaddles the baby. "Why don't you take your daughter out to the waiting room to meet her aunt and uncle?"

"You don't want to wait and do that together?"

"I think if you don't do it soon, Brook and John will shoot their way in here." She laughs as she hands me the baby.

I can't help the smile that's on my face when I step out into the waiting room. John and Brook are immediately on their feet, swarming around me.

"Oh, Jake, she's beautiful," Brooklyn coos.

"Congratulations, man." John slaps me on the shoulder.

"I want you to meet your niece, Blake Remington."

"I bet you won some brownie points with that name," Brooklyn says, taking Blake out of my arms.

"How is Zoe?" my brother asks.

"She's good." I pull him over to the side. "I need you to do me a favor."

"Anything, man."

"I want to marry Zoe today. Do you think you could find someone to hitch us?"

"Are you sure that is what Zoe wants?"

"There is no doubt in my mind. I've already asked her."

"I'll need to make some phone calls." I stop him before he walks away.

"Did Brooklyn get you up to speed on Knox?"

"Yeah, and I'm kind of glad you didn't kill him. He's going to get exactly what he deserves in prison."

Brooklyn hands the baby back to me. "Thanks to Knox, Zoe and I have found the cure for Alzheimer's. Too bad he will never get his hands on it."

EPILOGUE

Jake

"Hey, John. Did you read the paper today?" The screen door slams behind me. I hear the kids laughing in the playroom that Brooklyn had added on for them. "John! Where are you?"

"In my office," I hear coming from down the hallway.

The smell of cigar burns through the air as I get closer to him. "Man, Brooklyn is going to have your hide for smoking a cigar in here." I wave my hand in front of me, fanning the smell.

He holds a tightly wrapped Cuban in the air. "I think we have something to celebrate." I take it from him and sit in a well-worn leather chair across from him.

"So you did see that the bastard finally died."

"Knox will never harm another person."

"It took long enough for him to go insane. After his trial two years ago, I thought he'd lose his mind a lot quicker. Especially when Brook and Zoe's cure worked, and he knew he'd never have any part of it. Did you know that old bastard petitioned the court to collect money on the cure? Saying without him, we still wouldn't have the cure for Alzheimer's?"

John hands me a lighter. "Yeah, then he tried to buy the cure, and he was blocked from that too."

"He got what he deserved." I suck on the end of the cigar until I see the bright orange tip.

"He did, and it feels damn good to know that we are finally free of him. Part of me has always thought he'd come back for us." He props his feet up on the desk and leans back in his chair.

"I'd say our lives turned out pretty damn sweet. We both have beautiful, smart, sexy wives who have always had our backs, even when things went to shit."

"Hell, Brooklyn never backed away from the beginning. I don't know what she ever saw in me, but I'm glad she let her heart rule over that feisty head of hers. I would have probably been working for Knox until the day he died."

"Nah, you were already wanting out. She gave you the kick in the butt you needed." I place the cigar in the ashtray. "As for me, if you would have never met her, well...I'd be dead. Cancer would have killed me years ago."

"I guess we are both lucky she found me."

"We are, but my life wasn't complete until Zoe crashed into the picture."

"Did you ever figure out how you got into a bra and makeup?" He chuckles.

"Even if I did, I wouldn't tell you anyway." I laugh with him. "Speaking of the girls, where are they?"

"They've run upstairs to get their swimsuits on and to grab the kids' suits."

"Mmmm...Zoe in a swimsuit." I stand.

"You've got it bad," he snorts.

"What? I love that pregnant belly of hers. And who are you to talk? You can't keep your hands off Brooklyn."

We hear the girls call the kids to come outside. Like typical brothers, John and I race to the windows so that we can stupidly stare at our wives.

"God, she is so beautiful. I love watching Brooklyn with L.J. and Jack." John leans his forehead on the glass. "The kids are getting so big. Jack looks just like her mother. There is no way I'm letting her out of the house when she's a teenager."

"I think it would be wise to keep her away from guys like us." I snort. Zoe sees me watching her, and she shimmies out of her cover-up. I swallow hard and have to rearrange my jeans. John catches me and shakes his head.

"Having a little problem with your minion?" He roars out loud.

"Shut up!" I snarl. "My minion does just fine."

He laughs and places his arm around my shoulder. "I'm glad we're brothers, man, and that we've ended up with the perfect lives. Beautiful wives, great kids, and the Remington brothers together. What more could we ask for?"

***

Left to die. She destroyed him. He lives for bittersweet revenge.

Click here to purchase the first book in the series, Rebel's Retribution.

Falling Hard is FREE when you join Newsletter.

Thank you for reading *Hold Onto Me*. Your honest review will help future readers decide if they want to take a chance on a new-to-them author.

ABOUT AUTHOR KELLY MOORE

"This author has the magical ability to take an already strong and interesting plot and add so many unexpected twists and turns that it turns her books into a complete addiction for the reader." Dandelion Inspired Blog

Join Newsletter to stay up-to-date.

Armed with books in the crook of my elbow, I can go anywhere. That's my philosophy! Better yet, I'll write the books that will take me on an adventure.

My heroes are a bit broken but will make you swoon. My heroines are their own kick-ass characters armed with humor and a plethora of sarcasm.

If I'm not tucked away in my writing den, with coffee firmly gripped in hand, you can find me with a book propped on my pillow, a pit bull lying across my legs, a Lab on the floor next to me, and two kittens running amuck.

My current adventure has me living in Idaho with my own gray-bearded hero, who's put up with my shenanigans for over thirty years, and he doesn't mind all my book boyfriends.

If you love romance, suspense, military men, lots of action and adventure infused with emotion, tear-worthy moments, and laugh-out-loud humor, dive into my books and let the world fall away at your feet.

SERIES

Whiskey River West

Whiskey River Road

Elite Six Series

The Revenge You Seek

The Vigilante Hitman

August Series

Epic Love Stories

For more follow me on Amazon for a detailed list of books.

Or, on my website at kellymooreauthor.com

Made in the USA
Columbia, SC
22 December 2022

74860606R00135